A Hodgepodge of Reflections

Fictional Short Stories with an Academic Slant

by
Norma Wettengl

RoseDog ❦ Books
PITTSBURGH, PENNSYLVANIA 15222

The contents of this work including, but not limited to, the accuracy of events, people, and places depicted; opinions expressed; permission to use previously published materials included; and any advice given or actions advocated are solely the responsibility of the author, who assumes all liability for said work and indemnifies the publisher against any claims stemming from publication of the work.

All Rights Reserved
Copyright © 2008 by Norma Wettengl
No part of this book may be reproduced or transmitted
in any form or by any means, electronic or mechanical,
including photocopying, recording, or by any information
storage and retrieval system without permission in
writing from the author.

ISBN: 978-1-4349-9079-2

Library of Congress Control Number: 2008922984

Printed in the United States of America

First Printing

For more information or to order additional books, please contact:
RoseDog Books
701 Smithfield Street
Third Floor
Pittsburgh, Pennsylvania 15222
U.S.A.
1-800-834-1803
www.rosedogbookstore.com

When man on earth has done his best
    Let not the angels of heaven compete

For my beloved mother and father
Wilhel Lillian McGregor nee Silvera
And
Hubert Wesley McGregor
And
Their siblings

September 2009
Love & Best Wishes
Cherry   (NORMA WETTENGL)

Contents

A Turkey's Point of View   1

She Married Her Brother   11

Hardened Heart   39

On Visiting Hong Kong   47

My Father   53

My Mother   59

Sarah Comes Full Circle   65

Disillusioned Soldier   79

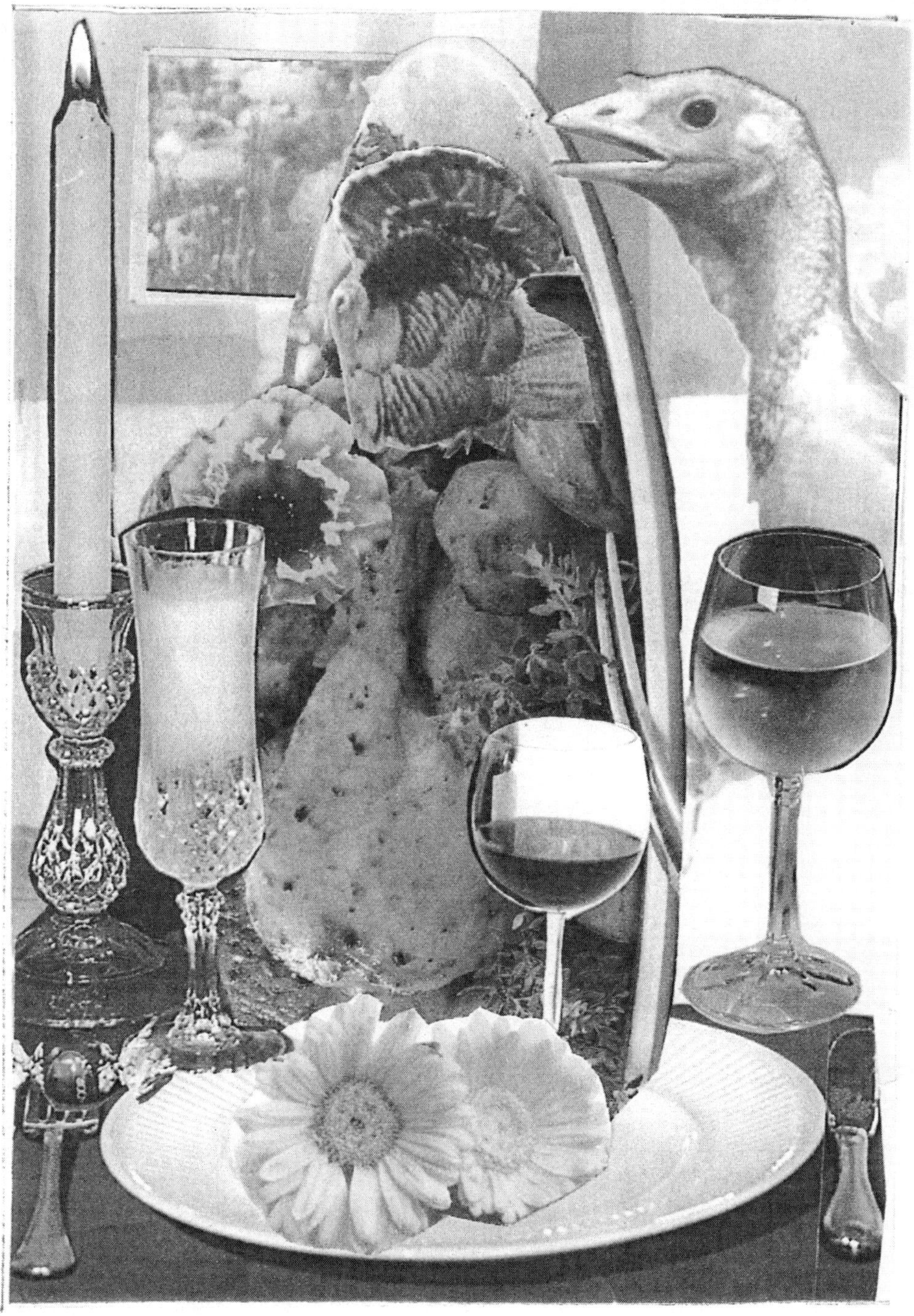

A Turkey's Point of View

The sun had dipped into the western sky and all that was left of its light was a violet-orange on the horizon when the Grants and their friends gathered to celebrate on the day proclaimed by Parliament on January 31st, 1957, as 'A day of General Thanksgiving to Almighty God for the bountiful harvest with which Canada has been blessed,'... and which day should be observed on the 2nd Monday in October.

The gathering was as fresh as a daily bath, and second-best-outing clothing prescribed the order of dress in a room as bright as its lights and as odoriferous as the smell of a roasting turkey.

Stuart and Carmen Grant and their twin daughters were milling about in the kitchen making ready for Thanksgiving Day dinner while keeping an ear open for the doorbell and the arrival of their first guest.

On such an occasion as Thanksgiving, the warmth and attention a guest receives on arrival through the door, is remarkable. For fleeting moments all eyes and smiling attention are on him, and never for the rest of the celebration will he experience such a feeling of warmth and welcome.

Stuart answered the door to let Nicole and her son Scott in. Nicole burst through the door with enthusiastic chatter, guffaws of laughter, and her heaving voluptuousness; Stuart responding to her greetings with his characteristic low-key politeness.

Nicole was cuddled into Carmen's warm embrace and pecked on the cheek as though the ladies had not seen each other in a long time, while Stuart attended by helping her to remove her light jacket, lingeringly hanging it in the closet. Just momentarily had Stuart allowed his gaze to be caught by her deep cleavage and the fullness of her bosom pressing against her v-necked sweater. He also refrained from staring overly long at the jiggle in her bottom as she walked towards the kitchen to join the party.

Nicole's full figure was a powerful signal of fertility, and therefore, linked to her sexual attractiveness. We are hardwired to appreciate those features of the female figure that are related to fertility; and needless to mention that youth is a potent ingredient of the fertility-mix. No doubt Stuart had always found Nicole to be attractive, and this was one of the many secrets he kept from Carmen.

Nicole, a divorcee and single mother of a son, was the nurturing type, who loved herself and all creatures under heaven. With her love and nurturing, her son Scott had grown into a socially well-adjusted lad whose graciousness and impeccable manners charmed all the celebrants. Like Mother Teresa, Nicole would give the shirt off her back to feed the poor. Nicole felt the pain others endured, because she knew the pain of relationships and loneliness. Her childhood lacked the security of belonging to a real home and the unconditional love of parents. As a result, she had developed a dark side to her outwardly sunny disposition and her empathetic concern for the needs of mankind: and that was her coquetry and exaggerated need for validation. For this reason she had grown into a harmless flirt, which nature had in the past, frequently thrown Stuart into a state of embarrassing confusion.

Nicole also loved food, and it was left to be seen how she would manage to avoid overeating on fat-producing foods in her effort to prevent weight gain. Whether she would eat some pumpkin pie, and if she did, whether she would refuse the whipped cream topping, would be concerns of personal importance to her. Unfortunately, Thanksgiving Day dinner is one of those events that present the temptation to overeat of the plentifulness of the fare.

Nicole, as was customary for guests to do on invitation to a dinner party, brought a token of her gratitude, and presented her hosts with a bottle of Magnotta, 1997 Vidal Icewine. "You had better put this in the deep-freeze for quick chilling," she said. "It should be served at six to eight degrees centigrade, otherwise the taste will not be quite right. Not to let it freeze, however."

Stuart was quick to follow Nicole's advice as he was wont to do after twenty years of marriage to Carmen. He had grown like a well-trained dog, willing to please his mistress. This was not as difficult for Stuart as you might imagine, since he was by nature a yielding peacemaker. It had become a part of Stuart to fade himself in and out without being much noticed. If someone broached a subject, he could take it up, though never with passion. By then, he had mastered the art of swimming with the current. Carmen on the other hand, considered herself important enough to display her talents in front of other people. She was vital, energetic and openly opinionated, and Stuart was no match for her in these departments.

A Hodgepodge of Reflections

Mariana, an old friend of Carmen's, was next to arrive. Mariana, who herself hardly ever drank of alcoholic beverages, and only half-heartedly approved of its consumption by any living creature, brought something she deemed healthy instead, and that was a box of mandarin oranges. Carmen, accepted the gift with great tact: "We all love these, and I assure you, they won't last long around here. The twins will demolish them one after the other, until they have all gone:" Carmen had spoken from the heart.

Carmen, of course, took charge of the seating arrangement, while she told nonchalantly of the change she made this time around to the recipe for the stuffing: a recipe Nicole had given her some years back. Carmen was a gifted cook who never followed a recipe faithfully, but would add or omit ingredients of her choice to create a flavor that was uniquely hers. This year she had added a granny Smith apple and a handful of raisins, which addition proved to be an ingenious touch. Carmen was artistic, and she strove to be creative as well as exceptional. This time around her table setting was indeed very special.

Mouths were watering, eyes were widening to sharpen their focus as they passed over the attractive table setting, —— over the Brussels sprouts in white sauce, the buttery mashed potatoes, the cranberry sauce, sweaty candied yams, and steaming whole-wheat buns, the warming gravy having been perfected by the connoisseurs with the utmost effort —— to rest on the main object of their desire: the roast turkey on its back, with legs spread apart as though to expose its parts that were once private, directly opposite the view of the host Stuart, who was to take his seat at the foot of the table.

The most capable and gracious host, Carmen, voluntary commander in chief of all proceedings, was to be at the head of the table, opposite her husband.

Between Carmen and Stuart, was an invisible mound of disharmony and minor irritations, all stemming from personality conflicts, and that had built up between them over the years they had been married. Carmen's antennae were permanently up to receive her husband's reactions towards her demands, and her claws poised to defend her position. She had grown resentful of what she considered his weak instinctual drives to take the initiative, to develop projects and carry them through without her suggestion and insistence. Her experience was that he got nothing done without her intervention, and that his laid-back approach to matters was frustrating. It is quite likely that Carmen's bossiness might have been brought out to the surface by Stuart's behavior. For every step Stuart made backwards from Carmen, she moved forwards one step toward him, until he was backed into his metaphorical shell. Stuart retreated from her into his secret double life, of which she knew nothing, and which knowledge would not only have surprised her, but deflated her bubble of security and self-assurance.

Up to that point, Stuart had been back and forth from the brink of infidelity, particularly with women younger and more attractive than Carmen, but his advances never materialized into anything more than flirtation due to a lack of a serious attempt on his part. This was his way of venting his pent-up anger and getting even with his wife without putting his marriage at major risk.

In his marriage to Carmen, he had found himself torn back and forth between strong wishes for fusion and a deep-seated wish for autonomy. But he was to find the solution to this issue of ambivalence, when he discovered a way to his own centre, out of which he could meet Carmen without fusing with her. As marriages go, theirs had the chances for survival, if it was never to hit the highest mark of success of total compatibility. Moreover, the marriage was strengthened by the common interest they shared in their beautiful and well-adjusted twin daughters.

The turkey was the main attraction of the celebration, and took center stage on the dining table, and spoke to the guests: "I know you have come with great expectations to have a piece of me, and that your hostess has taken all diligence to ensure your eating pleasure of my flesh and stuffing.

I have come a long way from my wild-turkey past and roaming free over the land inhabited by the First Nations Peoples, and later, around the mid seventeenth century, from my introduction to the first English colonists, —— and their Pilgrims amongst them, —— who had established the first permanent settlement at Plymouth in Massachusetts.

On a Cuddy Farm in the U.S.A., in the year 2005, I was hatched in an incubator from an egg made fertile by the method of artificial insemination, and was sold as a beautiful day-old poult to a farm in Canada where I was raised, free-running in a barn without individual identity, for the sole purpose of blessing your Thanksgiving table.

Having reached a desirable weight on the farm, at the tender age of sixteen weeks old, I was shipped to a slaughter plant where I would meet my destiny. I was transported along the conveyor belt of operations, sorted and tested by the authorities, and ended up in a supermarket as a whole, frozen, young and butter-based turkey. Needles to say, I was quite unaware of the proceedings that took place after my immobilization by electric current."

His speech falling on indifferent ears was muted by noisy chatter, and brought to an abrupt end by the whizzing sounds of an electric carving knife expertly handled by Carmen, who, once again, had usurped her husband's traditional role of turkey-carving. She alternately smiling and seriously carving, later discreetly portioned the sliced turkey meat and the stuffing into three lots, as was the practice: white meat, red meat, and stuffing. Stuart in the meantime, busied himself with the serving of wine.

Mariana was not to partake of wine, requesting a soft drink in its place. She wanted, however, of both white and red meats as well as some stuffing.

Sitting beside each other, to one side of the table, were the identical twin daughters, Dolly and Denise, celebrating their last year of acceptability for dressing in identical outfits. The girls up to then, had always enjoyed playing out their intentional plot to confuse strangers having problems telling them apart, or recognizing their unique identity. Today they were to set off a train of thoughts in Mariana's head, who was sitting opposite to them at the table.

Mariana looked across the table to the twins, both smiling mischievously at each other, exposing a full set of white and even teeth. Even their smiles seemed identical as well as synchronized, she thought. She was immediately struck by the glow of their facial muscular firmness and the sparkle of their youth. The image of her own face confronted her, and the contrast between youth and old age played around in her thoughts for a while. She concluded without a doubt, that the young were intrinsically beautiful, and that it was indeed a pity that they did not normally recognize this to be a fact. Sort of wasted on them, she figured. She thought they were normally preoccupied with what she had grown to regard as trivialities, and quite unappreciative of the blessings of their youth.

Mariana had given up her youth in exchange for experience and wisdom, both of which the young twins were in short supply . She had mastered the art of living and coping with joy as well as sorrow, and knew on all levels, that life was no longer a match for her unfathomable resource. On this occasion, she looked bedraggled from sleepless nights of tossing and turning in her bed, trying to find a comfortable position in which she may fall asleep. Some twitch or dull ache anywhere in her body, was the cause of her discomfort, stemming from osteoarthritis in her spine, where troubled facets and joints were exerting a pinch on spinal nerves as they passed out into inflamed and painful muscles.

Mariana was aware that her medical problem started the day she was born, and that it had taken seventy four years to have gotten that bad: that the condition could probably have been delayed, or even averted, had she a road map of her life showing the pitfalls and how to avoid them: with perhaps, something as simple as extra helpings of spinach or broccoli, or by the use of iodized table salt.

She voiced her opinion, giving some credit to the thought that: "our pain may be self-inflicted as the harsh medicine prescribed by the physician within us, to heal us from sickness," taking the opinion to a level of speculation.

Stuart presented a more realistic and natural reason for pain: "Pain is a warning of something gone wrong. It is a cry for help by the living body constantly striving for fitness —— constantly striving for survival." There was a pregnant hush around the table while everyone agreed in silence with what Stuart said.

This evening, however, Mariana's pains and aches would soon subside, as pains do when the mind is distracted away from them, only to return as soon as one tries to clear the mind for sleeping.

Nicole's newborn curiosity in the making of the wine she had brought, peaked with all that talk about it. The Icewine was a welcome conversation piece, as not everyone had heard of it. Not only was it a novelty, but its fruity, ice-cold sweetness were lingering flavors that demanded mention.

Mariana was more than happy to tell what she knew of it: "The fully ripened grapes of October are left untouched on the vine under protective netting until they freeze in the cold of December and January, at which time the grapes are arduously hand-picked and pressed. The juice yield is relatively low because most of the frozen water content of the grape is left behind in the press as ice crystals," she explained.

Everyone followed with interest and fully understood why the wine was so sweet.

On the subject of wine, Stuart braved a remark: " I understand that the daily glass of red wine is a powerful antioxidant, and is, therefore, good for you."

Carmen responded with an attitude: "And that is something he'd like to believe."

Mariana's tongue had been loosened and she gave it free reign: "Today, the consumption of alcoholic liquor is almost synonymous with partying, and the practice, now deeply entrenched into society, is not only habitual, but highly acceptable and desirable."

"This craving for the substance might be coming from the unmistakable thrill human beings get from breaking the law; whereas that certain regard for the unlawful —— instilled in the human psyche and passed down to us through the generations —— has come to us from the days of bootlegging of the product," Carmen theorized, smugly patting the coil of hair at the nape of her neck.

Nicole, helping herself to mashed potatoes, expressed her thoughts on the subject: "Then there are those amongst us who entertain the notion of invincibility, gambling with their health by drinking to excess of alcohol, despite their full knowledge of its harmful effects on the health."

Carmen, fixing her bun once more, expanded on Nicole's opinion: "One can become addicted to the habit-forming drug to such an extent, that cessation causes severe trauma. At this stage, one is described as an alcoholic. Alcoholism, a sickness like depression, can only be fully understood by the afflicted."

"Or at least one who has experienced such an affliction," Nicole added.

Mariana cleared her throat in preparation to say something else on the topic: "Moreover, we do like to be taken from the familiarity of our existence to a level of consciousness where we can lose our inhibitions and experience a new freedom of expression: and alcohol can do that."

At this point, there was a pause during which the topic seemed exhausted, before Nicole, in a high-pitched voice, added: "I do believe that some men who sip beer from the bottle at parties, are actually holding on to an image of masculinity, while the ladies who balance wine glasses at the stem, are actually savoring a feeling of sophistication."

There was a frown on Carmen's brow as if she disagreed. But Stuart was quick to support the concepts voiced by Nicole and added: "Hidden under these practices, may be found deep-seated feelings of insecurity. Much the same can be said for people who balance cigarettes between their lips or blow smoke rings."

Mariana raised her head to confront the dazzle of bows and buttons from the twins fashionable clothing. Becoming self-conscious of her own shabby clothing, she folded her arms defensively across her chest in an effort to hide her dowdiness. She felt like a floppy, threadbare sack, sitting on her chair. This image of herself was soon dismissed, however, as she grasped the opportunity to rescue Scott from his floundering attempt at telling a 'turkey' joke.

Scott, sitting across from his mother, was fumbling embarrassingly for words and seeming to have forgotten his lines, when Mariana seized the opportunity to fill in and embellish the story line with the full practice of her years: "Asked to write a composition on what he was most thankful for on Thanksgiving Day, little Timothy wrote that he was most thankful that he was not a turkey."

Mariana regained her composure relinquishing her floppy-sack image, and began to hold her ground for the rest of the evening. She shone brightest when helping people by supplying the lines they missed, the names of actors and authors, the parts they played, and the famous lines they wrote: she had a good memory for such things, and had earned the ridicule of being referred to as a 'walking encyclopedia,' or alternatively called 'Mrs. Brains'.

Dolly and Denise had been politely monosyllabic throughout the evening up to the point when Denise cleared her throat, gathered enough courage to tell a 'turkey' joke: "What do turkeys like to eat for Thanksgiving? Nothing! They are already stuffed."

And Dolly, who was not to be outshone by her sister chimed in: "What did the mother turkey say to her children? If your father could see you now, he'd turn over in his gravy."

"All crazy," said their mother half-embarrassedly, in lieu of an apology for what she feared were her daughters' feeble jokes, despite the polite and gracious responses to them by the party attendees.

Steve, a co-worker of Stuart's and friend of the family, sitting to Nicole's right and next to Stuart, had little to say for the relatively short time he was in attendance, during which time he paid full attention to the matter of getting his dinner eaten. His arrival and his departure were as unobtrusive as his presence. He seemed preoccupied, and left early giving the excuse of having to attend to an urgent matter.

Carmen explained to her guests that the urgent matter to which Steve referred: "concerns his son's involvement in an automobile accident. Steve's 2001 Honda Civic has sustained a write-off."

Nicole observed that: "Steve was quieter than usual. I guess he was troubled about having lost his car."

Carmen piped up, by way of an explanation: "Steve is always quiet, he's really shy."

"Surely, there's often a difference between being quiet and being shy," Mariana chimed in. "Which is it in Steve's case? Shyness," she continued: "can be symptomatic of a troubled upbringing of the young. Growing up, for example, with dysfunctional parents who fail to build confidence in the child. Self-evaluation, and ultimately, the worth of his opinion on matters, sinks to a level below normal, to the point where he loses freedom of vocal expression. Society labels him as being shy. He continues to live his life in the comfort zone, to find small solace in the hope that some may confuse his silence for underlying strength, or even a sense of superiority."

"Mariana, you have gone off on a tangent: I'm not sure whether Steve is genuinely shy or just suffering from a deficiency in his upbringing," Carmen was quick to half-defend Steve.

Mariana would not let the matter rest: "there are those with normal upbringings who have nothing to say through ignorance!"

"Ignorance has never stopped some people from speaking freely," Nicole added, surprising even herself.

No one responded to Mariana's observation, and the topic seemed put to rest as silence fell over the table; which silence was to be broken by Carmen offering second helpings of turkey, and, Stuart getting busy with a wine bottle.

Stuart was not saying much. He had secretly hoped to escape from the women after dinner, to occupy a remote corner of the house, where he could engage Steve in shoptalk: the way that men at mixed home-gatherings traditionally segregate themselves to a comfort zone of affinity, where they can share common interests during conversation. Stuart will, however, place himself in a safe place away from the small talk, and from possible confrontation, occupy himself with the serving of pumpkin pie and coffee. After which he'd scrape the plates clean of leftovers and stack them in the dishwasher.

Denise dropped a piece of food to the floor that had first fallen from her mouth to her lap. This made Carmen immediately aware of Woo's absence from the dining room. Carmen had been conditioned to think of the dog whenever food fell to the floor.

Woo's absence from the room afforded the twins a convenient reason to leave the dining table, to escape adult dominance, and perchance, to sneak a peek at the TV downstairs, while they went in search of the dog under the pretence of concern for its well-being. They once again moved in unison as they jumped up from their chairs as decorously as fan dancers, proceeded to run down the stairs leading to the basement with steps that sounded simultaneously rhythmical and competitive.

Woo, the short-legged French hunting dog with pendant ears and sad, bleary eyes reflecting an undefined sadness, was found napping on the floor in front of the fireplace, having taken leave from his customary position of hankering for scraps that may perchance fall to the floor by the foot of the diner.

In the girls' absence, Mariana, having achieved a free flow of chatter, slipped into her complimentary mode: finding the turkey to be done to perfection, the stuffing exceptional, wanting to obtain the recipe for the homemade pumpkin pie and having to examine the label on the cranberry sauce bottle for the sake of reference. Never was a guest so gracious and so full of gratitude in the house of the Grants. Like the taste of wine is remembered when the color is forgotten, and the vessel is no more, so will Mariana's graciousness burn like a flame in the hearts of her hosts and outlive the night.

The twins, aware of their duty to return to dinner in due course, were soon drawn to doing so because of the boom of festive cheers they could hear growing in volume upstairs. They returned to fine outstretched arms reaching across the table to hit wine glasses with those of others. In this round of cheers could be heard expressions such as "here's to you", "health and happiness" and "good luck on your exams;" and other such sweet sentiments as there were participants cheering each other.

The spirit of the cheers soared to the ceiling, filling the room and all the hearts therein. Feelings warmed to loosen the tongue and sweeten the word, to unfold the arm for touching and caressing. Despite all the differences between members of the gathering, they were now of one spirit in the sense of the following poem:

No man is an island.
    If he be a hermit,
he may wish to be alone,
but not to rid the earth of mankind.

No man is an island.
    If he be human,
he may deny the truth,
that he another needs.
  So let's get together and celebrate:
Give thanks for the bounty of the harvest
  under the banner of Thanksgiving Day.
Give thanks for the meeting of the old and the young,
    of the contented and the disgruntled,
    of the healthy and the sickly, all!
All, under the banner of our need for fraternity.

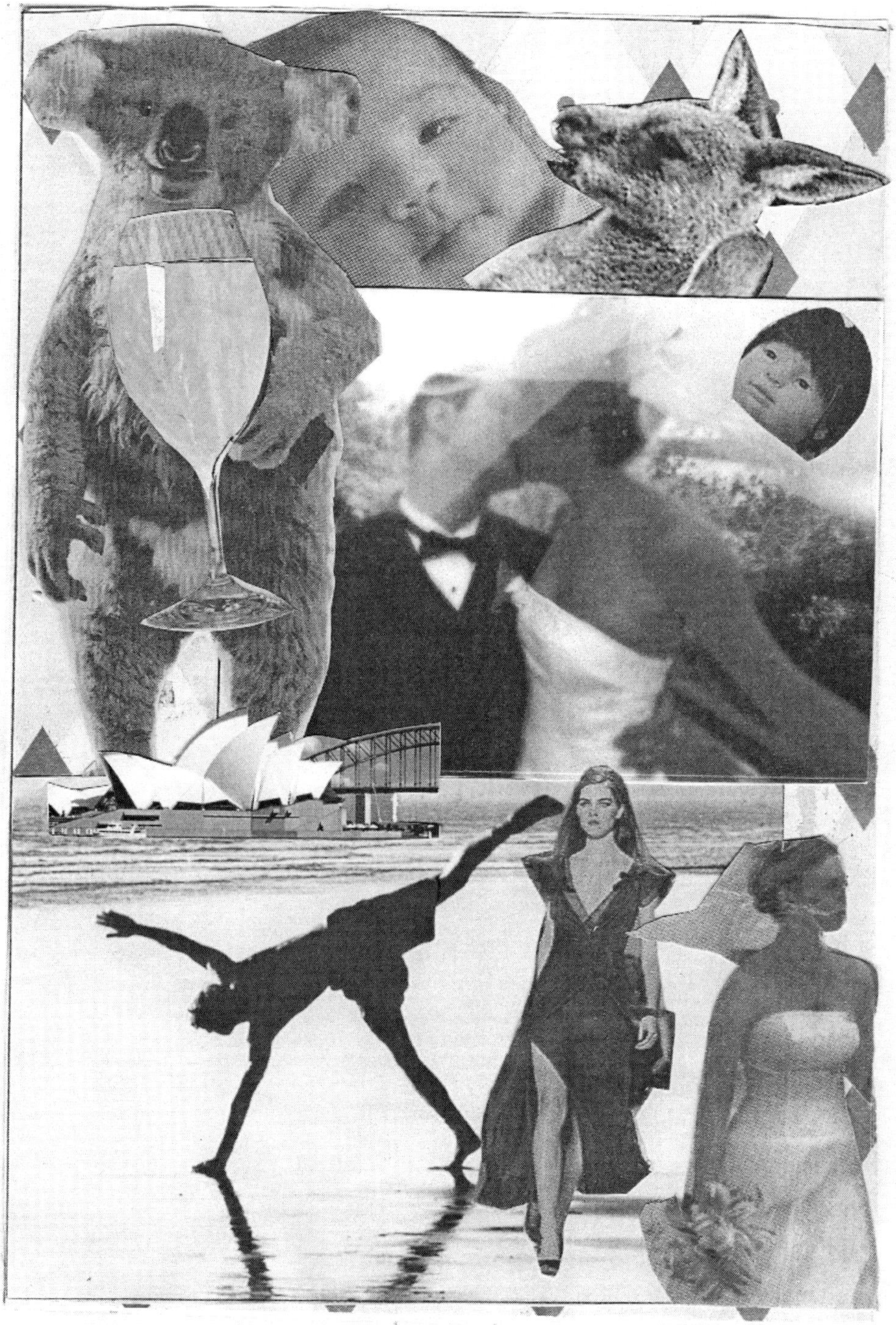

She Married Her Brother

Kate Wood was a dimpled child of Capricorn with a smiling sun-sign potential, and all there was of sweet seventeen in the year 1957. Indeed did she smile easily with strangers in her infancy, and would stretch her arms out to be lifted into their embrace.

With her Ascendant in Libra, her smiling disposition was no coincidence. Demonstrative, and just plain happy to be there, she radiated warmth and affection to all and sundry. Or so was her potential, until however, the astrological predictions of this mentally and physically normal girl were to be undermined by the forces exerted upon her by her immediate and extended environments.

The behavior of her parents, and the circumstances surrounding them, would play a major roll on an unusually sensitive spirit, infixing certain negative character traits in her personality that would prove detrimental to her full emotional well-being and overall best interest.

Rating herself as singularly unfortunate, Kate developed a complex concerning her mother Paula, whom she thought spent far too much time in bed simply nursing a migraine and a vague malaise for which there seemed to have been no cure. Furthermore, she perceived her as being sour-faced and angry, and largely overbearing in her method of chiding her: "You come straight home," she'd command, or "that's all there is to be said on the matter," would be the abrupt pronouncement in her attitude.

Her quandary began with her perception of the disturbing difference between

Paula and her closest cousin's mother, whom she viewed as being normal, as well as, up and about and full of life.

Undoubtedly, Kate's sensibility was bruised by her mother's apparent abnormalities and inflexibility, instead of enhanced by a kindlier approach in treating her daughter. Furthermore, Paula's constant complaining about her husband's shortcomings served only to add to Kate's irritation and derailment.

The dominant force to diminish all other forces working to undo Kate's basic nature, was to be found in the relationship between her mother and father. Paula and Tim always seemed on the verge of a separation or divorce. She witnessed many an outburst of arguments occurring between them, with Tim taking off and spending weekends away from the family home with his sisters living out of town. This unsettling state of affairs on the home front, failed to provide an atmosphere conducive to total emotional balance for an impressionable youth.

Even though Kate felt her father's love and caring for her, he was mostly absent from her daily activities, and the moments they spent together were perceived by Kate as light-hearted or superficial, —- decidedly lacking in inspirational quality and other solid aspects of fatherhood. Undoubtedly, Kate was deprived of the highest caliber of benefits a girl has to gain from a sound relationship with her father. Her potential was blocked on some level by the one who, ideally, should have been her dominant source of drive and direction.

"Hi Miss Puss! How are you little girl?" Tim greeted his daughter on his arrival home from work.

"Great Dad," she replied sweetly.

"Still hanging out with Nat Cole's Mona Lisa with her mystic smile, Miss Puss?" —- He was not a Nat Cole fan!

"Sure Dad. ... So you got a haircut eh?"

"Like it?" He asked.

"You are a handsome dude, ... Daddy dearest, everything suits."

"So what do you think of this yellow the painters are using on the walls?" He asked.

"I dig it! But shouldn't there be some white about to add contrast and soften the yellow blast?"

"I agree. I think your Mother is working on that. I'll try to catch some shut-eye before I leave," he said on his way over to his favorite armchair.

"Pleasant dreams Dad." Thus ended a typical chitchat between father and daughter portraying the average depth of their verbal exchanges. Never had he asked a question of this basically shy girl that enquired into her aspirations.

Kate's basic nature sought expression in the performance of her talents in the limelight. She wanted to be noticed, to be praised for her accomplishments. In the absence of opportunity for adequate self-expression, she resorted to negative attention in her mind, escaping reality and retreating into a fantasy world. Most importantly, she lost a part of her self-confidence and a voice to speak out on her own behalf. Self-doubt and a degree of inferiority complex, worked their way into her psyche.

Her admiration for those amongst her peers who were brave enough to hold an audience by telling stories, only brought her more self-doubting. She grew nervous about voicing her opinions and public speaking in general, thinking everyone else was better at this than herself.

She had always wanted to become a medical doctor when she grew up, but kept this career aspiration her secret, simply because she considered the desire lofty and beyond her reach, and did not want to appear silly by revealing it: despite the fact that she had no reason to doubt her mental capabilities since she had always placed within the upper third of her class in academic contests. More importantly, she felt deep within her heart she would not have received the emotional backing needed from her parents, and thus allowed her dream to lie dormant.

It was in the spring of 1958 that Kate graduated from high school with a B-plus average. This achievement waltzed into her sphere without hard work or a conscious design on her part to do well. She had only her native intelligence to thank and the fact that she allowed herself to follow the flow.

At the graduation ceremony, it was announced that she would be taking a year off before attending college, during which time she would consider optional courses of study, spread her wings a bit, preferably to a place outside of Toronto. She had never felt the shores of Canada and lusted after lands tropical, white sands and palm trees.

During the summer of that year, the golden opportunity to visit her uncle in Brisbane, Australia, presented itself as a surprise to Kate, along with an element of fortuity. It was surely a stroke of luck that Tanya, her best friend, was able to sway her mother, an employee with Air Canada, into obtaining a special ticket for her so that she could travel to Brisbane via Hong Kong at a greatly reduced price. Tanya herself, was happy at the prospect of having found a suitable travel companion in her best friend.

Tanya, curious to find out more about Kate's Australian uncle Robert, asked: "So what's your uncle really like?"

"He's much like Dad, easygoing and fun loving. Because he's not my dad, I can tolerate these qualities more in him. It's alright to be like they are, but my dad does not recognize there's a needy side to me. Uncle Robert is an aircraft mechanic with Qantas Airways. He has done well for himself, really! In his job and all. He's a single guy, and I'm not sure whether he has a girlfriend or not."

"Is he handsome?" Tanya queried.

"Very good looking. Even better looking than my dad, —- I think! —- I feel he'll allow us some freedom. That's what we want, right?" Kate was pleased to add.

"Well! I sure wouldn't want him to be strict."

So full was Kate of keen anticipation, she could hardly endure the wait before her planned departure for Brisbane. She found, however, that the days before their departure to Australia went by rather quickly, as days do when pleasant anticipation rules.

They arrived in Brisbane late in the night of January the 5th, and awoke in the morning excited to investigate their new surroundings. They awoke animated by what sounded like shrill laughter and mimicking bird chatter coming from the lush vegetation of their neighborhood. They later learned that the chatter, mimicking the human voice, came from the cockatoos, while the laughter, carrying a note of mockery in its delivery, came from the kookaburras. It was an awakening like none other they had experienced before.

The carcinogenic and skin-damaging sunshine flooded their beings like a warm liquid. The girls were soon to be intoxicated by the warm embrace which would put them in the mood to follow its lead. What seemed like eternal sunshine in sunny Brisbane, led them into a nearby park and across the train tracks until they came upon a bus stop with a bus sitting in it that was marked 'downtown.' In a snap, the girls looked at each other, and in the language of silent agreement, they jumped into the bus through the open door rather hurriedly, before its engine started.

The feeling of adventure put smiles on their faces that beamed all the way into the city center. There, in their most carefree of moments, like the ones that prompted them to board the bus, they entered a door with a sign promoting palm reading.

Zahra the palmist looked shriveled with age, but the light in her eyes lit up the small and dark room that was barely big enough to hold the three of them sitting around a small and round table. Alternating skepticism and curiosity kept the girls spellbound throughout the reading session.

After the readings, Kate related to Tanya what the palmist saw in her hands: "There's one thing she told me that rang a bell. Looking in both my palms, the left and then the right, she traced the imaginary arc made by the four fingers where they join the palm, stretching from the Jupiter finger (index) to the Mercury finger (that's the little one), she observed that my arc was not ideally smooth, but that it dipped down off course where the little finger joined the palm. She described this marking as having a low-set Mercury finger. Amazingly enough, this is how the finger develops on a child who suffers stagnation of self-expression under the influence of her parents or guardians. This child faces a difficult approach to life due to a restricted ability to communicate in person, especially if displays of affection are called for. Do you think this is why I find it difficult to talk to strangers and to hug someone I'd like to hug? However, on a brighter note, she also saw a marking that indicated a latent gift for written communication and advised that I should be very successful in undertakings of writing."

"Perhaps. That's really far out! No wonder you got such good marks on your English assignments. She didn't see you meeting Prince Charming on this trip?"

"No. But she saw me coming out of the closet into the open to reveal a cherished dream of mine."

"Really! Any idea what that might be?"

Kate was silent. Sufficient unto the day was her revelation thereof. She hoped privately that the dream the palmist alluded to, was the one of her wanting to become a doctor.

"So, what is all this hocus-pocus Zahra the palmist was up to?" Tanya said reflectively.

"Not nonsense", retorted Kate. "She explained that the lines in your palms actually represent myriads of nerve endings that are ultimately connected to the brain. A thought pattern, or habitual behavior, can actually change the quality and direction of a line over time. Even a change in diet can do that."

"That's amazing!" Tanya responded, a bit abashed.

"Couldn't she have seen how many children you'll have?"

"No. Only one's physical and mental states, or potential, can be interpreted by the markings of the palms. Only those aspects of fortune bound to one's physical or mental make-up can be predicted by interpretation."

"Too bad, I wish you no less than a charming prince on a white charger." Tanya said flippantly.

"So what now, should we take the bus we came on, back home? It certainly won't be marked 'downtown' anymore."

"Let's phone Robert and see if he can pick us up."

"I'd rather get home on my own steam. Let's take a cab and share the cost." Kate was emphatic.

The next day, the girls were pleasantly surprised to find out that Robert had taken the day off work in order to take them to the seaside on Bribie Island.

Having arrived at the beach, once they braved the water on entering the surf, they found themselves resisting wave after wave with the full force of their bodies, with no time between successive waves to regain a firm footing on the destabilizing undertow. The struggle with the unrelenting waves did not allow them the opportunity to get swimming. Nevertheless, with a spirit of adventure and the challenge posed by the waves, the girls turned what could have been a turnoff, into amusement.

Pictures of the sea Kate remembered being drawn to, were the ones she had seen in photographs and magazines, where sunlight passes through calm water to the ocean floor, to shine right back at the sun with its intricate meshwork of lights. So though the trip to the beach was educational and entertaining in its own way, it presented a different picture of the ocean than that preconceived by the girls.

As deserted as the beach was, Robert happened to run into friends of a sort, neighbors of his, that kept him out of the water with chatter, much to the surprise of the girls. His neighbor was having a yard barbecue party in a couple of days, to which he invited Robert and the girls to participate.

Robert warned that his neighbor's parties were usually on the wild side, ending up with loud buffoonery due to tipsiness, but that they were also renowned for an abundance and variety of food, as well as, an array of interesting people from all walks of life.

"Lots of interesting people eh! That's cool. Perchance a knight in shining armor will emerge from behind the Tee trees to swoop you off into the sunset," Tanya said with a goofy gesture of a hand and raised eyebrows.

"If he does appear, you can have all of him to yourself." Kate's retort expressed sarcasm.

"Now we get to wear some party clothes, at last!"

"And all that make-up we lugged across." Kate added.

There's nothing like the prospect of a glamorous party to spark the fancy of a young girl. She sees reflections of herself in the mirror of her mind competing with each other in search of the prettiest one of them all. She'll settle on one image of herself and strive to portray it in dress. Finding the ultimate outfits for the party was a compelling challenge with which the girls became intoxicatingly preoccupied.

A concern of the girls that there might not have been any attendants to the party within their age-group with whom they could identify and mix, was put to rest when they discovered that a satisfactory handful of suitable teenagers and other young guests were present.

The girls soon overcame their initial uptightness, and began to experience a warming cordiality with their new acquaintances. Kate found Sean Whylie in particular, a young man four years her senior, to be most agreeable and physically appealing.

The attraction between Sean and the girls was mutual. It was no surprise that the evening did not end without Sean extending an invitation to show the girls something more of the city.

The sexual attraction between two people is complicated and multifaceted. A pattern present at birth, if not in the womb, and ending with life itself, will unfold itself during growth and maturing. The unfolding of this predetermined pattern is largely shaped and colored by one's exposure to the multitude of external influences imposed on one by one's environment. Surely, influences imposed on Kate began in her home environment.

On some level, Kate regarded her original source of parental love as weak, and in her estimation, neither parent as providing a positive role model she was inspired to emulate. This loss of love, real or imagined, and her need for a positive self-image, created a void within her which led to a yearning to recapture that which was lost or denied. New sources of love were created in her imagination, and directed toward the outside world.

This appetite for love becomes, and will remain insatiable. It becomes impos-

A Hodgepodge of Reflections

sible for anyone to satisfy her hunger with his love. The subject, through no design on her part, must hold onto sadness with the need to punish the wrongdoers who withheld their love from her in the first place. She will, subconsciously seek the wrong partner, one who can only bring her frustration. The partner to whom she would be attracted, would be one who promises to fill her need for approval and, at the same time, one who promises by her intuition, no solution to her dilemma.

Because Kate's self-worth was on the lower side, she was wont to lose interest in anyone who displayed a serious amorous interest in her. He could not have been up to standard if he considered that she was worthy of him, would be the rationale behind her judgment, and the reason for her action. Her interest in an admirer would have lasted only as long as his actions remained illusive, during which time she would strive to prove her worthiness for his full commitment.

The following poem, composed by the author, illustrates the concepts of the preceding paragraph:

> I asked that he love me true, and he did.
> I asked that he love me forever, and he tried.
> True love forever, came too easily, and that was hard for me to take,
> So I asked that he leave me lonely, and he did.
> The bitter-sweet rejection was mine to endure, and hard for me to take,
> So I turned to another,
> Asked that he love me true, —— that he love me forever.

"Tropical rainforest! That doesn't sound like fun to me!" Tanya exclaimed giddily.

She, of course, was referring to the planned excursion to the rainforest under the leadership of Sean Whylie and his friend Martin.

"It's not the expedition that I'm interested in, but the guide." Kate was smug.

"I guess I'll have to settle for Martin, then." Tanya was always agreeable.

"Come on! We'll share them both."

"So you say," Tanya said, yielding the right oh to a friend.

The girls were pleasantly surprised to find a rainforest stuck almost on the outskirts of the city centre: a few hours drive away from it.

The girls were drawn into the reality of the eerie magic of the rainforest that they had experienced before only in words or pictures. Kate grew apprehensive of the low-lying mossy limbs of trees appearing like gruesome hairy arms reaching out to touch her in the face. She soon grew accustomed to looking up in order to avoid them and, alternately looking down to the ground in order to sidestep the boggy patches underfoot.

So went the trek through the amazing growth of giant ferns, trees and fungi, until they completed a circle, arriving at the spot where they entered the maze, with some surprise at that knowledge.

Not only was Kate impressed with Sean's knowledge of the flora and fauna of the rainforest and his masterful guidance through it, but she was elated by feelings of conquest, having completed the hike she initially considered an undesirable undertaking.

Throughout the trek, it was as though she and Sean had gone in different directions, unmindful of each others presence, but in the end, wound up completing the hike and arriving together at the place they entered the forested maze to find themselves face to face. Kate stood mesmerized by the impact of Sean's presence, and found herself blushing behind her dark glasses.

Kate had closed not only a circle through the rainforest, but one of emotions as well, beginning the day she was first attracted to Sean at the barbecue party, and ending in the completion of the trek through the rainforest. Feelings she could not put into words, amounted to more than mere physical attraction.

At this point, native bashfulness kept her from making eye contact with Sean, despite the sudden flood of emotions she was feeling toward him, and that was kindling her desire to make physical contact with him on whatever level was his bidding. She was in the mood to indulge the passion she was feeling, with a certain sense of abandonment, that came with the knowledge that in the event of any ensuing disappointment she might encounter by engaging in a fling with him, would be cushioned by the geographical separation between their two worlds, as soon as she returned to Canada. She knew nothing of the ramifications of carrying out a long distance relationship, and the notion of engaging in one had not entered her head.

Little did Kate suspect that distance would not put an end to her involvement with Sean: the memories of him would dog her footsteps into her future like shadows phasing in and out somewhere in her background.

However, there was one important ingredient missing from her mixed bag of emotions: and that was the knowledge of Sean's feelings toward her. If Sean had reciprocating feelings toward her, he, like her, had not let on. The jovial chumminess between Sean and the girls, coupled with the fact that he had shown keenness in keeping in touch with them, sufficed to bring Kate a small measure of requitement.

Subconsciously, Kate was being drawn into the intrigue of following her heart, under the dictates of her quest to love recklessly. She must relentlessly pursue his affections up to the point where she wins them. Only with the overwhelming evidence of his serious intent would she have abandoned her chase, after having been turned off by the revelation of his devotion. She played to win, and winning would have brought her the loss she craved.

"Hey! Sean phoned while you were out. He's inviting us to a farewell dinner at his place next Tuesday in our honor. It's up to you." Tanya had taken the call.

"That's great! Sure, I'd love that. That's two days before we leave, … that's cutting it tight. But who can resist!" Kate's dimpled beam reflected her delight.

A Hodgepodge of Reflections

The merriment of the farewell dinner was replaced at leave-taking by expressions of sentiment as the girls became tearful. Light-heartedness was not all washed away, however, as the good-byes did not express finality but rather the hope of meeting sometime in the future.

Holiday blues slowly replaced fatigue and boredom in the gorgeously dressed up girls, as they tried hard to conceal their low spirits, en route from Sydney to Toronto.

Kate was overcome with mixed feelings of wanting to return to the only life she knew, and not wanting to give up that intriguing bit she had just experienced in an exotic land where life was carefree and fun-filled.

She likely would have given way to tears under the pressure of despondency, if it were not for the comforting presence of her upbeat friend sitting next to her. With all the inclination she could muster for day dreaming, she found herself entertaining a resolve to return to Australia using the savings she'd stash away from her measly employment earnings.

Kate voiced her thoughts and asked a loaded question: "Would you like to return to Australia?"

"I might want to live there, eventually," was Tanya's surprising response which puzzled Kate as to the source of her motivation. She would have been certain of hers.

"Let's both return for a longer holiday, get under-the-table jobs to support ourselves for six months, and see whether we'd like to live there," was Tanya's bright idea.

"Maybe we could attend university there and eventually work our way up into citizenship. We have eligible sponsors!"

Tanya had a nagging curiosity to satisfy: "Where did you and Sean disappear to at the farewell dinner party?"

"He was showing me family pictures," Kate said sheepishly.

"Just wondered," Tanya said, refusing to appear too nosey.

"Would you get in touch with Sean if you returned?"

"If I didn't, it wouldn't be because I didn't want to." Kate was deliberately sidetracking.

The love-game between Kate and Sean will remain a contest that ended in a tie, as neither one of them capitulated to a confession of strong feelings, despite the obvious sparks that flew between them. Kate knew how she felt, but she remained uncertain of his inner feelings. It is without a doubt, that a part of Kate will remain unfulfilled by this outcome of her uncertainty.

After two short days of their return to Canada, the girls returned to their respective part-time jobs and took up pretty much where they left off.

Despite the absence of an expectation to return to a change on the home front regarding the circumstances between her and her parents, Kate's mood was dominated by a seething undercurrent of agitation. She was finding it difficult to settle down from the spin the Australian holidays had put her in. She wished to return into the groove from which she left: to redirect her focus to familiar projects and activities, and to find her old self.

Her anxiety to establish a normal momentum in her life, threw her into a state of physical lassitude, which resulted in her decision to pay a visit to her doctor. The medical examination addressing Kate's complaints was routine and unrevealing of any specific cause. On the grounds of this finding, she was asked to return in two weeks, if her symptoms persisted without sign of improvement.

This was the doctor from whom Kate had sought to obtain a contraceptive device behind her mother's back, three years prior. Since it was not acceptable for medical practitioners to preach morality to their patients, it was not in her doctor's place to recommend abstinence as an alternative, and the only foolproof method of avoiding pregnancy. She had, however, suggested that she use the condom.

Little would Kate have expected that in the space of three years since her clandestine visit to the doctor, that in 1960, the U. S. Food and Drug Administration would approve the first oral contraceptive drug for marketing in the U. S., and that in 1963, the Ortho Pharmaceutical would introduce the first Pill. The Pill was as easy as a pop, more reliable, and more satisfying to the users than the less invasive condom, which at the time was the most popularly used of contraceptives before the introduction of the Pill.

It was only in 1892 that the Canadian parliament made contraception illegal, and that, that ruling resulted in the notion that the providing of information on contraceptives to a woman was scandalous and even illegal.

Kate was not to return to her doctor to follow up on her post holiday feelings of dejection, as she was winning the fight against the blues.

Kate's period was one week late on February 15th, 1959. She was not concerned during the first week of lateness, for the reason that since her menarche, she had experienced irregularity in her menstrual cycle. When three weeks passed, however, and her period had not appeared, a new concern took over. She was smart enough to realize that she should have seen her doctor to investigate the reason for the lateness. However, her habit of keeping secrets, especially from her mother, also kept her away from the doctor.

Today, Kate would be able to test herself for pregnancy using a 'home pregnancy test' kit obtainable from her supermarket. The test she could carry out in the privacy of her home without anyone being the wiser. Home pregnancy tests can detect the presence of the telltale hormone, Chorionic Gonadotropin in the urine, as early as the first day of a missed menstrual period. She needed it at a time when pregnancy testing required medical assistance.

Kate unwittingly was avoiding the stress and terror of testing and waiting for

A Hodgepodge of Reflections

the results of an unwanted pregnancy, with the full knowledge that her decision to do so was not only uncourageous but foolish. This conflict within the girl pushed her deep into denial, where she clutched onto the thin hope of chance to reverse or deny the worst outcome.

Wallowing in self-denial, and searching for explanations for the cessation of her periods, Kate took temporary solace in the recollection of the adult conversation she once overheard as a younger child, touching on the menstrual disorder, menorrhea, (halting of the menses), which usually took place in girls, and the mentioning that a change, such as going on a vacation, could have been a possible cause of that occurrence.

In a state of preoccupation with her pregnancy concerns, Kate searched frantically through her mother's Medical Encyclopedia with warranted curiosity, to find that the cessation of her menses was the only symptom she was showing. The fact that she was not experiencing morning sickness during the first trimester, brought only small relief as she gathered that not all pregnant women suffered this symptom.

Continuing to finger nervously through the pages of the encyclopedia, the possibility of a miscarriage loomed into the realm of her conceivabilities. She read that as many as fifteen to twenty percent of all pregnancies result in miscarriages nearly always resembling an especially heavy menstrual period. She found it interesting, that in addition to a number of medical conditions, miscarriages could also be caused by vigorous exercise.

Thus a routine of energetic activity became a priority in her life. She would run instead of walk, hop, skip and jump about unnecessarily, stretching and twisting her body with unprecedented vigor and frequency, ... all to no avail. This engagement aimed at bringing about a possible miscarriage of a dubious pregnancy, was failing miserably. She was distraught.

At this point, a subconscious need to unload the burden of her secret, prodded her to pick up an invitation to go swimming with her friend Tanya at the local community pool, on which occasion, she hoped the beans would get spilt one way or the other.

"Are you pregnant?" Tanya blurted innocently, observing from sideways the slight protrusion of her friend's tummy, just above her bikini line.

Kate's mouth flew open as she went white with the shock of realizing that her pregnancy was already observable. She swallowed her heart back into it's rightful place. She managed to get the words out with an equally casual voice as that in which the question was posed: "Why do you ask?"

Tanya might be flippant, but she knew a thing or two, and was actually a bit more worldly than Kate.

"Just asking, as your tummy looks a little fat."

The moment of truth seemed too tense for both the girls to bear. So, Tanya swam away from the uneasiness towards the far end of the pool though bursting with native inquisitiveness: a quality both the girls had relied on in the past to solve many a problem. She returned emboldened by the recollection of this truth, to satisfy her curiosity and continue her query.

"So, who may the dad be?" Assuming Kate had affirmed her suspicion!

In the meantime since the pertinent, though shocking question, was posed, Kate was feeling the need to confide in Tanya and reveal her unbearable secret to her.

"I'm sure you can guess," was all she said, relying on her best friend's intuitive trait to come up with answers.

"Does he know?" Tanya said cautiously.

"For Christ's sake! No! I know nothing about him! Don't even know whether he's married or alive."

"And don't tell me! You haven't even seen a doctor!"

"Would you go with me? Soon!"

Kate could not believe she had actually reached this crossroad in such a short swim.

The girls sat across from a concerned Dr. Potter. Kate's pregnancy had progressed into the second trimester. Her pregnancy was unwanted, she was unmarried, young and lost, and her unborn child's father was no where in the picture. There was little room to paint a grimmer scene.

Having nothing to lose but desperation, Tanya braved one final question: "is there a chance she could get an abortion. Is there someone you could refer her to?"

"Not in the second trimester. No doctor would touch her with a long pole, for fear of having a run-in with the law. I could refer you to an adoption agency if it ever came down to that. Anyway, think about it, and let me know how I might help. I'd love to continue being your doctor."

The grim girls left with the grim news as though Kate had just been handed her death sentence. She could have bawled her head off, if it were not for her preoccupation with the wagging index fingers of Folly and Carelessness chiding her to her face.

From about 1850 through 1945, abortion was restrictive almost universally. The effect of these prohibitive laws was to direct those seeking abortion procedures to illegal practitioners at a high cost in maternal distress or fatality. It was in 1869, that the Canadian Parliament had enacted a criminal law which prohibited abortion and punished it with a penalty of life imprisonment. It was only ten years hence, after the occurrence of Kate's pregnancy, in 1969, that the Canadian abortion law was liberalized to permit some therapeutic abortions to be performed in hospitals.

When it came to helping a friend in need, Tanya was not one to leave solutions up to chance, but to take matters into her own hands. Having come to her wits end in her mental search for answers, she in desperation, and with the full knowledge that her action would not have met with Kate's approval, decided to seek the advice of her mother, and thus perchance benefit from her larger experience.

Tanya using a somewhat indirect approach said: "So Mom, I have some surprising news for you!"

"What is it?"

"Kate's about four months pregnant!"

"You are kidding!"

"No, she and I went to see Dr. Potter yesterday and she told us that."

"Tell me, does Paula know?"

"Can you imagine Kate keeping that secret from her mom so long! Crazy girl!"

"I mean it! I want to talk to that girl immediately, if not before. Get her over here. I want to talk some sense into her. If not, ... I'm sorry Tanya, ... if she doesn't tell her mother, I will."

Her mother's stance lifted a load off from Tanya's shoulders. In silent assent she was pleased with the outcome of the revelation, even though she was shaking in her shoes about the whole incident.

Two weeks passed, and Kate had not gone to see Tanya's mother. She was so afraid of what Paula might do in reaction to the news. Entering a fit of rage, yelling a string of abusive words, was the course of action she anticipated from her mother. She actually felt she would have preferred that she be told by Tanya's mother, so, she chose to wait for that to happen.

It was not easy for Tanya's mother to gather up herself for the pivotal telephone contact. But it was her duty she felt, and she lost no time in carrying it out.

The shock came to all concerned, and mostly to Kate of course, at Paula's reaction to the news of Kate's pregnancy. Paula was not herself. She was observed to have acted out of character. It was as though she had gone through a transformation: ... gone melancholic, ... or changed into a zombie. She was almost frightening to witness.

Paula's experience was that she was shaken from terra firma to an underwater place where she hung suspended, as she reached out for Kate in one embrace encompassing the nineteen years of her daughter's life. She became immersed in the recognition of motherly love she had never before experienced. Her movements were seen to be slow, vague and other-worldly as she sobbed tears that were baptismal.

Kate, overcome by what she interpreted as her mother's deep concern manifesting itself in a strange display of affection for her, began to sob uncontrollably within her mother's embrace.

Paula emerged from her bizarre experience to find Kate sobbing in her embrace, and both mother and daughter covered themselves in tears of resignation to the reality of their predicament, and the recognition of a new beginning to the course of their lives.

During the coming weeks, self-inflicted shame and blame kept Paula soul-searching beneath her new cloak of docility. She went through the motions as though she were still in a trance. She had no need to hold council with her conscience about what she wanted to do about Kate's pregnancy. She was fully resolved that she wanted to proclaim her grandchild to be hers. Her husband, Kate's father, she vouched was wont to uphold her decision, he being a man with a submissive nature and a keen sense of family.

This arrangement, agreed upon by Kate and her parents, would allow Kate to pursue a life as close to normal as possible, and thus free her of the encumbrances of single parenthood.

In life, it sometimes takes what one perceives as a personal calamity to jolt one from one reality into another. It remains up to one whether he manages to make good of the perceived catastrophy handed to him by life. The Woods had entered into a new reality with the resignation to making the best of their perceived misfortune.

Today, the Woods might have taken a different attitude toward the whole affair. They may not have suffered needless shame in the reality of illegitimacy taking place in their midst. The stigmatization of illegitimacy, a feature of the Victorian period and its characteristic fastidiousness in morals, is today not only inapplicable but ludicrous. Human resistance to this Victorian attitude over the years, has brought about a reversal, to the point where illegitimacy is today not only acceptable, but openly practiced among the popular and admired crowd.

The Woods, however, were caught up in the hangover days of that period of time, (1837-1901) : a time when mothers of children born out of wedlock were alienated, humiliated and economically victimized in the effort to discourage the practice of bastardy, which was regarded as immoral behavior.

It was not until the latter half of the 19th century that the Victorian sense of social conscience slowly recognized the need for reform. Though reform moved slowly for fear of violating the Victorian ideal of the sanctity of the family, at the close of the Victorian era, the battle for the protection of infant life and a more equitable law regarding the financial security of illegitimate children, was mostly won.

Regardless of the new philosophy regarding illegitimacy today, it is not what the Woods would have wanted for Kate at that point of her girlhood life. And more importantly, it was not what Kate wanted for herself.

Devious was Paula's scheme to take over Kate's baby. She and Kate would leave town surreptitiously to live quietly in Montreal under the pretext of having accepted an invitation too good to pass up: to work as a mother-and-daughter team in a scientific research project that presented a unique opportunity for a pregnant woman. Which pregnant woman would have been Paula herself. She did not elaborate on the details of the plan, just mentioned that an ailing uncle of hers would provide free accommodation and keep, in exchange for domestic duties while they were in Montreal. After the birth of the baby, they would return home with the claim that the child was Paula's.

It was accepted that a number of local people on the home front would come to learn of the truth. How far and wide the truth would spread, and what repercussions would ensue would always be a concern of the Woods. Nevertheless, they took solace in the thought that out in the world at large, as well as in matters legal and important, the cover-up would remain secret.

While in Montreal, Paula having been shaken up and landed into a new reality concerning her relationship with her daughter, found herself becoming increasingly amenable and willing to communicate with Kate. Barriers previously understood to be impenetrable, and that separated Paula from Kate, crumbled imperceptibly, giving way to the development of a new relationship between mother and daughter, closely resembling that of sisterhood. Doors to each others inner core of secrets were opening up. Most remarkably the door to the secret Kate had carried around closest to her heart for years, that of her wanting to become a medical doctor.

Despite the mountain of things the Wood women had to do in order to set up a functional life style in the city of Montreal, they found themselves in surprisingly good spirits. This upbeat frame of mind came to Kate having discovered the side to her mother that was capable of unconditional caring for her happiness.

Looking wearily at the abundance of kitchen gadgets lying on the kitchen table and counter yet to be put away, the words came fluently from Kate: "Did you know that since I was about six years old, I've wanted to become a doctor? She paused to put away a small strainer in a drawer, and afterwards glance at her mother to observe her reaction to what she had just disclosed, then resumed talking: "I once started telling my dad when I was about nine, but the phone rang and he never returned after taking the call, and I have never mentioned it since."

"Kate, I had no idea! I'm happy to learn that. Often wondered what you were going to do with that good brain God gave you. ... By all means at my disposal, ... a doctor you'll become!"

Kate's heart was warmed beyond an immediate response. She gathered herself while putting things away hurriedly, then responded in a voice that betrayed a heightened emotion: "Well, thank you mother! For that vote of confidence. With your assistance and moral support, I'll endeavor to be the doctor I've always wanted to become. But sufficient unto the day are the hindrances thereof, ... right? First things must come first. ... Right now, there's a baby to be had."

For the first time, in the awareness of what could someday become a reality,

Kate was beginning to harbor doubts and envisage pitfalls in her quest for her Holy Grail. She put the whole idea of wanting to become a doctor on the metaphorical back burner, nevertheless, allowing it to remain on simmering heat until the time in her future when she would return to pick up the challenge.

For the rest of the time Kate spent putting things away on shelves and into drawers, the memory of the prediction made by the Australian palmist regarding her deep secret that she would one day openly confess, filled her with the intrigue and mystery of that forecast. She dared to hope that the second part of that prediction, forecasting the materialization of that dream, would also be true.

Kate found it peculiar that Paula had not taken to bed with a migraine since their arrival to Montreal. Could it have been the shock of learning of her pregnancy that caused the disappearance of the disease from her mother's system, was the question on Kate's lips. She was curious and felt free to enquire: "Mom, don't you have headaches anymore?"

"I've been taking a new medication. It seems to be helping so far."

"Was it your mother you said, that had migraines? I sure hope I never get them. You have no idea how your poorliness got to me."

"It was my aunt Joyce that had them. It does run in families, you know! I think I have the common type. I understand sufferers of the classic type see auras of zigzagging lights, while some others display bizarre complications, including loss of consciousness, or even vision. ... So! ...There you are, I'm lucky!"

"So what's this new medication you're taking?" Kate's voice indicated that she was relieved to learn that her mother's migraine was not one of the more serious types. She wanted to hear more: "What causes them anyway?"

"Brain chemical imbalances. I was taking a nonsteroidal, anti-inflammatory drug that worked on the pain but not the cause. Now I'm taking an antidepressant to work on the cause, instead of the symptom."

"Great Mom! So do you have a new doctor?" Kate asked curiously.

"No, a new naturopathic perspective."

Kate ended the tete-a-tete with a rational remark: "Was it Shakespeare that said, all is well that ends well?"

Kate gave birth to a normal baby girl on November 20, 1959, after which event the ladies and newborn returned to Toronto with hearts full of gratitude for the very many things that went well during a time beset with precariousness.

Mother and daughter were too preoccupied with baby affairs to get fully caught up in the Yuletide spirit, and to a greater degree, in its activities. For them, the christening of Leah Wood, as the baby was named, was the highlight of the festive season.

The days for Kate went by slowly, while she bided her time making application to medical schools and awaiting acceptance to one of them. In September of 1960, she was admitted to the medical school of Queen's University in Kingston.

Kate, having vouched never to let another man interfere with her emotional stability, devoted herself to her studies, fitting into her spare moments the duties of a loving big sister to Leah, over a period of seven years. After graduating, she went on to specialize in radiology, and later served as a radiologist at the Oshawa General Hospital. A woman of the world, she had left home and taken a very nice apartment on her own.

Leah's true identity remained a dark secret, except to the few who through necessity had learnt of the truth. Tanya was the foremost confidant taking pride in guarding the Woods' secret, considering the entrustment of that guardianship, an honor and a privilege.

Leah, like Kate in her childhood, was of a sweet disposition. Unlike Kate, however, her personality was not exposed to the blemishing influences imposed by her parents and that caused Kate to become sullen and self-deprecating. On the contrary, Leah was allowed to become self-assured, well-adjusted and rather precocious for her years at any stage. Those who knew her, predicted only a bright future for her.

It has been observed, that grandparents tend to be more loving and lenient toward their grandchildren than they were with their own children, and this was certainly the case with Paula and Tim. Paula and Tim doted on Leah, gave her the emotional support she needed to blossom forth into the beautiful flower she became. Undoubtedly, Paula never returned to her sickly and sulky self she used to be before Kate became pregnant. And, as for Tim, he was as nice as ever with an added amount of detectable caring and involvement in Leah's activities. Both Paula and Tim had learned their lesson well, and taken it to a new level of parenting achievement.

The most influential character trait that Leah inherited from her biological mother, was her spirit of adventure: more precisely, the one that would take her away from the familiarity of her surroundings into the unknown of a foreign land.

Anecdotes related by a classmate of hers, portraying the neon brightness and bustling excitement of Hong Kong, inspired Leah to plan a trip to that city, to take place around her 18th birthday. Like her mother, she too had connections in the country she chose to visit. Her aunt Rosalie, Paula's sister and a grade school teacher with one of the English schools of that Foundation in Hong Kong, would meet her for the first time, provide accommodation and act as her willing chaperon.

Since Leah had no teaching experience, and no formal training in that profession, and indeed no higher education, her aunt advised that any application she might make from Canada for a teaching position in Hong Kong, would prove to be an exercise in futility. What she needed to do was just to arrive in the country as a long-term visitor, at which point, she would find it less problematic to respond to any of the many outcries for teachers of English from English-speaking countries.

Some employers may go as far as to intercede on the behalf of an applicant in obtaining a work permit in order to satisfy the legal requirement.

The challenge was for the taking, and Leah was game at the age of eighteen.

Three weeks after Leah's arrival to the exciting newness of Hong Kong, her aunt fixed her up with an insignificant, privately run preschool, where she was employed to help out on a part-time basis in exchange for her spoken English.

"This Saturday night, I'll take you … we'll all go, to a discotheque in Wan Chai. It's not really a dress-up thing, but you should at least look sexy." Leah's aunt Rosalie had decided to feed her niece's craving for the novel.

"That sounds like fun. Dress sexy! How?"

Rosalie opted to cast her a bait: "only if you want to compete with the millions of Philippine girls that will be there. Fit in with the rest of the swinging crowd."

"Only Filipinos will be there?" Leah's voice tapered off.

"Mostly, I'd say. A number of whites, and a few Chinese. But I swear to you, you'll find it different. Not like any dance you've ever gone to, where people prefer to sit around talking and drinking, and straining to hear each other over the music. While up for a dance, they let themselves go instead of remaining uptight waiting for the music to end so that they can find the closest chair on which to sit … something like playing musical chairs. Ladies here don't sit around waiting to be asked, … they just get up and dance, with, or without a partner. The crowd goes wild with fervor and rhythmic contortions. Dancers cover the floor, where everyone becomes a potential partner."

"Really! Sounds like my speed." The prospect filled Kate with anticipation.

Leah, having warmed up to the feverish pitch of the disco-madness, was soon attracted to a certain young man who she was finding it difficult not to follow with her eyes as he moved around the hall. He, as though through magical powers, had become a magnet to which her watchful eyes were drawn.

Leah, unlike her biological mother, was not one to play coy. She danced her way across the floor to perform a jig in front of her new captive, who, still dancing and smiling at her, switched his steps to competitive gyrations as he moved directly opposite his new partner. The moments they spent together for the rest of the evening were fatally enthralling.

Leah's chosen partner, Brent Miller, being fully aware of the effect his physical attractiveness had had on girls of his own age, was only slightly flattered by Leah's action, despite the fact that he regarded her action to be intentional rather than incidental.

So, through sheer involuntary action, Brent played the role he was accustomed to playing, engaging his admirer in chitchat. By the end of the soiree, Leah and Brent had exchanged personal particulars including that all important telephone number, with some expenditure of nervous energy.

A Hodgepodge of Reflections

Rosalie was surprised that Brent had chosen to drive his Jaguar automobile into Wan Chai, instead of taking public transportation that generally offered relatively cheap and efficient service, eliminating the exorbitant and unavoidable parking fees. She later learned that, that unwarranted spending would not have been one of his concerns. Not that he was by nature wasteful, but that his grandfather and his single mother were well-to-do.

This affluence of the Millers was evident in the size of the mansion in which they lived, and certainly in the elaborateness of its design. On entering the lobby of the mansion for the first time, one would have been struck by the enormity of the adjoining rooms and the luxuriousness of the carpet beneath his feet, as well as the grandeur of the curved walls and cylindrical columns reaching high up to the ceiling into a luscious growth of tropical plants. A winding staircase leading to the upper floor, was overhung by a gigantic crystal chandelier resembling the one used in Andrew Lloyd Webber's stage play: The Phantom of the Opera. Ahead and beyond, an expanse of the sea, studded with mountainous islands, viewed through a wall of glass, was the final display adding to the total visual delight and opulence of the Miller's mansion.

The Millers who were not born into money, viewed their new wealth as coming to them through hard work and a little bit of luck thrown into the mix. After the sudden death of his wife, Brent's grandfather took his only child April and her son Brent, from their homeland of Australia, to seek his fortune and a new direction to his stalemated life, in the foreign land of Hong Kong. His Hong Kong employer, unable to carry on with the manufacturing of goods in China for sale abroad, sold his ownership to Brent's grandfather, who, with his good managerial and entrepreneurial skills, eventually expanded the venture into a multimillion dollar business.

Frequent trips to China took him away from his home base in Hong Kong, while April on the other hand, having had taken over the duties of caring for her father and the household since the death of her mother, welcomed the opportunity to remain unemployed, in order to remain committed to fulfilling her father's needs and to caring for her son. Brent, was the outcome of a one-night sexual encounter with a man April deliberately failed to inform of his son's conception, birth, and existence.

The word that best described April was eccentric. The adjectives, effervescent, open and savvy also applied to this essential libertarian, who was physically small, neat and nifty. Eccentricity and dauntlessness could have been a harmful combination to someone less kindly in disposition toward her fellowman than April. Her sensitivity toward people's feelings, and her compassion toward the wrongdoer, would serve as her buckler against an ill-humored disposition.

She embraced the freedom to put comfort and what she deemed practical, ahead of fashion. For this reason she once chose to ride the bus wearing a wide-rimmed, straw hat and oversized dark glasses and no shoes on her feet. It was on a hot day, and her argument was that she needed to keep her feet cool, and the sun from her head and eyes, despite the concept that a lady would never be caught dead on a bus barefooted. Her freedom of spirit was often to be observed in the way she conducted affairs without regard for fashionable opinion and even acceptability.

It was with the same spirit of freedom that April kept her own counsel and found the courage to carry through with actions she considered unfoundedly stigmatized. This was the main reason she decided single-mindedly to have her baby Brent out of wedlock and to bring him up single-handedly.

In 1978, Brent left Hong Kong for Australia to study engineering at the University of Queensland. Leah, missing a friend in Brent and in her life, soon found good reason to plan a trip to Australia under the pretext of wanting to visit her uncle Robert in Brisbane. The fact that she needed to leave Hong Kong and reenter it in order to obtain a new allotment of time allowable to a visitor, afforded her the perfect excuse to leave the country. Not that Leah as known to all, would have needed an excuse to do what she wanted to do anyway!

The receipt of the generous gift of an open, round trip ticket to Australia from April, filled her with marvel at the realization that arrangements in life can indeed work out perfectly.

While in Brisbane, the desire to remain close to Brent inspired her to seek entrance to the university in the very program into which Brent was enrolled. His admittance to the institution, however, would not materialize until the following year.

With no shortage of money with which to purchase travel tickets, both Brent and Leah went back and forth from Hong Kong to Australia while the relationship between them grew steadily stronger, up to the point where they made up their minds to share an apartment in Brisbane.

The young twosome, Brent being five months younger than Leah, remained fully engaged in their studies with the financial and emotional support of their parents for four years, after which time, they decided to tie the knot in a simple ceremony that would include only their close relatives in attendance. Because they were young and unemployed, the couple agreed to delay having children until they were older and financially stable.

Leah's parents, Paula and Tim, and her sister Kate, arrived in Brisbane for the wedding with justifiable longing to meet Brent and his parents, as well as to reunite with Robert and other members of the Wood family they had not seen for several years.

Leah, wanting to make a one-time and lasting impression of lavishness on the Millers, talked Paula into a somewhat extravagant setup for Robert's ample back

A Hodgepodge of Reflections

yard, requiring a very large tent under which the wedding reception would take place. The tent would accommodate a stage for musicians and singers and an improvised dance floor. A number of friends, not present at the wedding ceremony, were to be invited to partake in the gay and sumptuous party to take place outdoors in an area to be decorated with cut flowers and potted plants to create the effect of an elaborate garden.

At a heartwarming family-get-together, Robert and his Canadian house guests, indulged in after-supper small talk, reminiscences of olden times and, not the least entertaining, gossip. Robert took delight in projecting onto a screen the many slides he had prepared over the years, and if those were not enough, showing them the pictures he also had in albums.

"You know uncle Robert, it has been twenty three years since I visited you in 1959," Kate said, wanting to engage Robert in reflecting on that unforgettable period of her life.

"How time flies. Look at you now! A bigtime doctor! The desire you sure kept under wraps, ... but never the potential." Robert chose his words carefully to carry a complimentary note.

"Has your neighbor been having more of those wild barbecue parties since I left?" Kate asked with nostalgia in her voice having never forgotten where she met the unforgettable Sean Whylie.

"Remember those wild and extravagant parties ... they just burnt themselves up." Robert was ignorant of the role the party played in shaping Kate's life. His voice lacked the sensitivity required to soothe her recollections.

Looking through one of Robert's photo-albums, Kate came across a group photographs in which she spotted Sean Whylie standing next to a girl that looked as if she could have been April when she was much younger. Kate never turned the page of the album. She froze on the inside, grappled with concealed fear that if her speculations were affirmed, they could only lead to an ugly unraveling.

She continued to show unruffled outer calm, and did not once, allow herself to get ahead of herself. She turned to Robert pointing at the girl in the picture, and asked: "Who is this girl?" As calmly as would have been normal.

"I'm not sure. She was at one of my neighbor's outdoor barbecue parties. I think she came along with the Whylies. I can't remember her name, if ever I heard it. Why do you ask?"

"She looks as if she could be April twenty three years ago. Of course you met April at the wedding reception, what do you think?" She moved the album closer toward him.

"You're right! She does look like a younger April. If not her look-alike."

Kate was disappointed that Robert was unable to verify her opinion. In a state of guarded anxiety, she clearly knew that she could not rest until her curiosity was satisfied.

31

Her thoughts raced through her head. On this trip to Australia, she had embraced the unlikelihood of running into Sean Whylie. To make contact with him now, or even to enquire after him, were definitely not on her agenda. She had decided to let sleeping dogs lie. For this reason, it was out of the question for her to ask him whether he knew the girl in the picture. Her mind next ran on Robert's neighbor as a source of the information she saught. He too was advisedly dismissed as a likely source since she hardly knew him, and furthermore, the undertaking would have presented elements of awkwardness on her part, and a logical mystery for the neighbor.

It became abundantly clear to her that April herself would be the one to identify the girl in the picture, if indeed it were herself. Regarding the prospect of getting to the bottom of the truth through April, she took comfort in the fact that she had always found her to be rather approachable and forthright. It was now imperative for Kate to arrange a meeting with April at the earliest possible time since she had only a few days left in Australia before returning to her medical practice in Canada.

The calm in Kate's life, created by the familiarity of circumstances surrounding it, was being threatened by gathering storm clouds and destructive winds, that would uproot and replace this calm with the uneasiness of uncertainty. Like a song that goes suddenly voiceless, her life had taken a turn into the unknown.

Should she ask Robert's permission to take the picture out from the album and thereby raise curiosity, or should she simply slip it out and into her handbag, in order to avoid explanation, was the question that haunted Kate. She had to have the picture one way or the other, and that was that, so she decided to take it from the album and just tell Robert she had taken it.

It was with a certain amount of trepidation that she invited April over to Robert's place, took her by the hand as she stepped out of the car, and whisked her away into the property shrubbery, saying she wanted them to go and look out for wallabies hopping about. This way they could do their talking without being overheard, she had concluded.

"This picture is from Robert's photo-album. Are you in it?" Kate asked handing the picture over to April.

April caught off guard, reached out for the picture mechanically, looked at it briefly showing more than a hint of recognition, said smiling: "That's me there," pointing to herself, "when I was quite a bit younger. Taken in Robert's neighbor's yard."

"And do you happen to know the guy standing next to you?" April was still looking at the picture.

"I sure do. We were lovers that night, after the barbeque. Sean Whylie. Why! Do you know him?" April's outspokenness pleased Kate, as she anticipated hearing the truth, and nothing but.

A Hodgepodge of Reflections

Kate's heart rate quickened, her palms became clammy with sweat, as a bad scenario unfolded to substantiate her suspicions. "I more than know him." She had summoned up the courage to be as outspoken as April was, feeling that the gravity of the matter required complete openness. "I too was his lover for one night." She pinched herself to check for the reality of it all, and to verify that it was indeed herself who was engaged in such outspokenness.

Had she opened up to divulge that Sean was the father of her child, there would have been a bit of explaining to do. Moreover, there would have been no need for her at this point to open her can of worms, never before uncovered, if Sean was not indeed Brent's father. She would wait to take her lead from April as to what she should say next. She was actually awaiting a confession from April that Sean was Brent's father.

"If it were not important, I would never think of asking. Of course you don't have to answer. But, whatever you say will be a secret between us. I promise. Is Sean Brent's father? It is very important that I know the truth." Kate's direct and pointed question came out timidly yet urgently from the depths of pure fear and extrinsic bluntness.

"I don't understand why you're asking this. No one in the whole wide world knows who Brent's father is. Not even Brent ... nor my Dad! Could you tell me first why you want to know?"

The fact that April did not straightway deny that Sean was Brent's father, which she easily could have done, and more than likely would have, only served to strengthen Kate's suspicions.

"It has to do with Brent's marriage to Leah. There is a possibility they could be brother and sister." As though in a state of emergency, Kate's words came from a place of desperation.

"Are you telling me that Paula had an affair with Brent's father, whoever he is?"

A frustrated Kate was concerned. She must break down and tell April that she was Leah's mother.

"Not Paula! I'm Leah's mother, and Sean Whylie is her father." This piece of information came as a shock to April, and the delivery of it, left Kate barely standing on both feet. Kate was left to come to terms with her surprising act of forthrightness. Her new-found courage to be open was engendered by necessity. Had she confessed too early and unnecessarily, if indeed Sean was not Brent's father, it would have been a disclosure she could not have retracted.

"My God! Tell me you're not serious. Brent has married his sister. Of course, there has to be DNA testing!"

Both women felt they had just stepped from the face of the earth into the twilight zone. What had they done to deserve this strange turn of events was a mutual and silent question. They remained void of feelings for a while, then drawing from their inner reserves of strength, they mustered the courage to face and deal with the obvious no-win situation.

The women, with capable heads and loving hearts, having arrived at a crossroad together, bonded in purpose to resolve a common predicament. It was imperative that they decide in a hurry to take no uncertain action.

"There's only one thing we can reasonably do, and that's to tell them." They spoke almost in unison expressing the same mind. Kate continued to speak, repeating the thought she had just voiced and agreeing with April: "Tell them, of course. It's not going to be easy, ... but it has to be done ... and soon."

So, without delay, they agreed to call a meeting including themselves, Brent and Leah, Paula and Tim in attendance. They would plan to meet for a picnic to take place in a nearby park. Brent's father would not attend as he had already returned to Hong Kong.

In the park where the involved family members would partake in the picnic of disclosures, a basket of cheese and tomato sandwiches was placed on a tablecloth spread out on the ground beneath a persimmon tree. The setting was both perfect and ominous at the same time. It was certain that eating was not uppermost on their minds!

Paula and Tim had been duly briefed as to the purpose of the gathering and on what had transpired between Kate and April. However, Brent and Leah had yet to hear the earthshaking truth. Both will have to face the staggering disappointment and the inevitable dissolution of their marriage, while Leah had to come to terms with feelings of betrayal by a grandmother and a biological mother who, since her birth, pretended to be her mother and sister, respectively.

Paula prudently volunteered to open the exchange, by first confessing to Leah that she was not her biological mother, but that Kate was, and how she, in a sense, adopted her from Kate in order to allow Kate the freedom to pursue her girlhood ways of living without impediment. At this point, Paula took hope in the thought that as soon as Leah was able to live down her hurt and betrayal, she would forgive her for her obvious error of judgment having kept Leah's identity from her for such a long time.

"So mother dearest! ... grandmother, or whoever you may be, it took you twenty three years to tell me this. Why so long! ... Mother! Did you think I couldn't have handled the truth before now? And you, sister dearest! ... Mother, or whoever you are, you went right along with Paula for twenty three years. How could you have?" Leah's voice betrayed hints of both disappointment and anger. With her head bowed in disbelief, her facial expression had progressed from smiling to serious and downcast throughout Paula's revelation.

Kate felt compelled to speak up in Paula's defense, to express gratitude and admiration for what she deemed was Paula's noble action of taking her child and the responsibilities of parenting, at a time when she herself was but a mere child: at a time when illegitimacy would have proved shameful for her and her family as well.

Leah, feeling left out of the support campaign staged by Kate for Paula, forced herself, for the sake of olden times and a genuine admiration for her mother, to add: "I can't complain about your maternal virtues, Mom. I just think I should have been told earlier, that's all."

Leah's impasse with Paula and Kate, concerning their deception and their overly long delay in telling her the truth about her rightful parents, dominated the atmosphere so far. Little did Leah realize that the bigger disappointment had yet to rear its ugly head over the course of the family conference.

April who had been a silent listener up that point, despite her forthcoming nature and high tolerance for the astonishing, was at a loss for words, or other response, to what she had just heard from Paula and Kate. The time was now ripe for her to tell of the part she played in the ongoing saga: "Listen up, I have something you'll find hard to believe. You all know of course, that Brent was born out of wedlock, and that I raised him without a father. He does not know his dad. To cut a long story short, Kate got a hint from a photograph as to whom his father might be. So, we got together and we discovered that both our children were fathered by the same man."

"How can you be so bloody sure Mother?" Brent's first vocal input was charged with outrage. "I want to get his name and whereabouts! We must have blood tests and DNA work done, immediately! What an unholy mess!" Brent felt it was only a short while ago that he was happy, and how suddenly he found himself trapped into unhappiness with his newly acquired relatives that he actually knew so very little about. Never before had he viewed them as strange strangers, with a story stranger than fiction.

Up to this point of the conference, Brent had not made eye contact nor spoken to his wife. He had not wanted initially to interrupt the flow of the conversation nor to upset its delicate momentum. In his heart, however, he wanted to let Leah know that he loved her nonetheless, and not one jot the less.

Brent stood up melancholically, ... chin almost touching his chest, ... excused himself from the gathering: "Excuse me, ... I'll take a short walk, I'll be right back," his voice trailing lamely after him as he walked contemplatively down the slope, one step in front of the other, never to return. He had excused himself from an unbearable situation, and being unable to clear his head, decided not to return to the discussion with muddled and downcast thoughts.

Brent's words and physical display of anger, were not indicative of a remedial concern for the impact the revelations would have had on his marriage to Leah. Nor did they indicate concern for what Leah might have been feeling at the time. His immediate response was one of venting his anger: which emotion superseded these concerns, and diametrically opposed a consensus of his opinions.

Leah was in mental agreement with Brent that there had to be scientific confirmation of their relationship to each other. Her thoughts took her back to the time she was watching a movie in which a father and both his daughters were run over by a truck and killed on the spot. She had tried her hardest to put herself in the mother's shoes, to feel what she was feeling, knowing very well she couldn't get it right. For the first time since then, she was getting an inkling of what the death of a loved one might mean to a loving survivor. She knew in her heart that, that loved one was Brent, even though he was very much alive. The sadness of losing a loved one through death, was to her, akin to losing Brent through an unfortunate turn of events.

Overpowering emotion rendered her incapable of tears: she closed off her feelings to those around her. She decided that she and Brent needed time to recuperate, to sort their lives out from emotional entanglement.

The tragedy was defined by that which befell Brent and Leah, even though their actions in the drama were irreproachable. All the actors in this tragedy had acted with the best intentions toward their fellow players, and though no one could be honestly blamed for the part he played, he must now live with the consequences of his actions, if not his involvement.

Life had thrown one of its inescapable monkey wrenches into the path of the couple's young lives to disrupt its even tenor. It was up to them to overcome this hurdle. The strength to be derived from that endeavor, would come in aid of any future effort to surmount obstacles yet to crop up in their lives. The strength gained by overcoming today's trying experience, if once faced with courage and fortitude, will only serve to increase your resistance in surmounting tomorrow's obstacles.

Thus the saga came full circle to where it began with the leading lady's mishap of becoming pregnant at too early an age, forcing her to give birth to a child out of wedlock, followed by a sequence of events leading up to the marriage of her biological daughter to her half brother Brent.

The following poem depicts Kate's frame of mind at the time of her pregnancy living under the influence of her environmental circumstances that made her do what she did:

    Concepts of herself over time ——
    Set in stone, and in her being ——
    Cemented all she ever knew, to her present,
    Became the force behind her choice.

    Her heart could only play second fiddle to her pride,
    And proud Pride, having found a partner in Prejudice, swayed her vote.
    Her heart could only play second fiddle to Pride.

A Hodgepodge of Reflections

But concepts born of Pride, ——
Like the stone in which they're set ——
Will yield to the wear and tear of human protest,
Until they crumble with time under the surge of resistance.

Only then, can man look back and see
The absence of Pride where it once stood,
See it today, —— in a new place of ridicule and irrelevance.

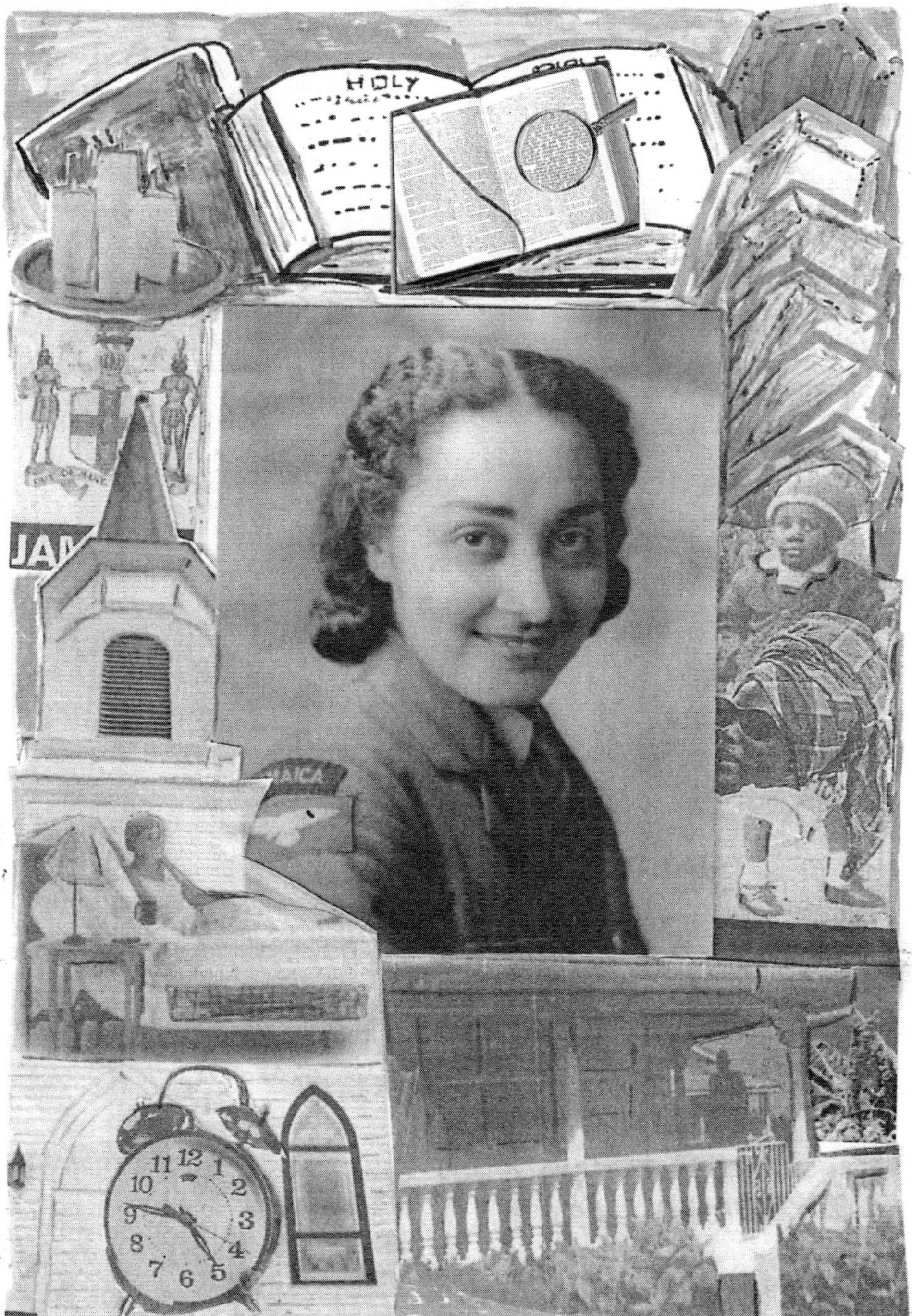
HOLY
BIBLE

Hardened Heart

The woman was waiting in a queue of churchgoers by the exit door of the church to receive the customary greeting and handshake from the pastor, who incidentally, had just delivered a lively and heartwarming sermon touching on certain aspects of the afterlife, and which had had the effect of putting a definite shine on the woman's countenance.

Forthwith, my curiosity to observe this woman, led me to follow closely behind her on the way out of the church to the bus stop, where my curiosity grew into a compulsion to further investigate her individuality.

To avoid the embarrassment of watching her in the presence of others who could observe my impertinent inquisitiveness, I drew upon my ability to transform myself into an invisible being, from which state I set out to indulge my curiosity.

I observed her entire body bound by a network of tight-fitting nerves in the exact places that her skin covered her, so much so, that the network and her skin were one and the same: (indistinguishable as separate to the naked eye), and that this network, besides emitting a dull glow of electricity surrounding her, completely occupied the entire space that the rest of her body occupied at the same time, for wherever in her body she was pricked, she would always feel that prick. This curiosity of a substance fully filling the space occupied by another substance at the same time, such as can be further illustrated by the relationship between the body and its network of blood vessels, can be explained by the microscopic nature of the network systems.

In these respects she was not unique, except for the sensitivity of her nervous system and the condition concerning her heart. Her heart it appeared, had obviously been pulled in several emotional directions along garden paths of her youth that led to frustration, and its strings, tugged in painful directions by admirers and lovers of her unique attractiveness. There was the well-bred Calvin Norton with his lovable sense of humor, and later there was the somewhat suave storekeeper, Mike Azan, both of whose advances at wooing the woman were brought to abrupt ends by the behavioral oddness of the members of her household. She had already come to terms with spinsterhood, having painfully learned to abandon her cherished desire to marry and bear children.

The minibus service in rural Jamaica was notoriously irregular, so there was no telling whether the woman had just missed a quick succession of buses, and would thus have had to wait a long time for the next bus to arrive. At the bus stop, as she blurted out some enraged criticism about the bus service, I was not surprised to find that the aura I first observed surrounding her had dulled the moment she decided to walk home having grown impatient with the long wait for the bus. However, the prospect of walking some thousand steps home under a tropical midday sun, brought sweat to her forehead, while the gleam the church sermon had put on her face, yellowed into a choleric flush. Not all the gentle breezes coming across from the sea in the distance to cool her skin would prove adequate to bring her comfort nor a cheerful frame of mind.

I followed the short, thick-set woman's lead over the distance to her home, observing her swaying hips as she balanced herself on custom-molded orthotics, that pinpointed the reason for the bitter derailment of her career ambition of becoming a registered nurse, and established the reason why the nursing school's selection committee had rejected her as a candidate for success on the grounds of having flat feet. Flat-foot is a structural disorder in which the curve of the arch of the foot flattens: a condition that may cause pain with the excessive standing and walking to which nurses are normally exposed. The pain of this rejection, I detected in her to be the major frustration in her heart, and I reckoned it must have been greater than the total of all the pain she might have felt in her flat-feet had she served as a nurse. The measure of disappointment one endures when a vocation ambition is thwarted, must partly depend on the degree of one's passion of aspiration. Her mark of disappointment, was as large as her life itself, and permanently lodged in her heart.

As she ascended the driveway leading up to her front door, I detected in her the capability of imparting a feeling of strength to others, as was perceived in her energetic and forthright salutation to her neighbor. She left no doubt in my mind, that this ability came from her strong sense of justice and truth, and that she would always use it to address situations openly and directly. Her energy did not actually

A Hodgepodge of Reflections

come from anger however, as it appeared to on the surface, but from passion and a total commitment to truth, justice and an assertive approach to life. Early on in her life, she gathered the impression that the world punished soft tendencies, as it did in the case concerning her three older brothers who had not made a success of their lives having lost their inheritance through the absence of aspiration, a lack of insight and downright carelessness. So, their failure, in part, taught her to put her money on hardness, and to despise cowardice and softness.

Her hardheartedness came across in outbursts of passionately expressed criticisms directed toward the guilty or the blamed, while corrections were directed without hint of gentleness or compassion. Her nervous system was high-strung and conducive to her pattern of behavior, and I was not about to ask which came first; the sensitive nerves or the irritable behavior, as the answer would have been as evasive as that posed regarding the chicken and the egg.

On entering the home, she yelled a threat to buy herself a one-way ticket out of the country, for the reason that she found a saucer, from which the cat had drunken milk, broken in the middle of the floor. I could not have guessed what the circumstances surrounding the cat and saucer were, but such an outburst of rage must have come from a deep resentment towards things around her, and the loss of the saucer was likely to have been just another straw added to the camel's back.

There was something in the room however, receiving the energy from an incident from her past and that was drawing my attention to a number of framed photographs on the dusty whatnot. It was a photograph of her smiling, and dressed in uniform displaying a Royal Air Force insignia. I reasoned that the woman, being a citizen of the British Commonwealth, must have served in a British airplane factory during World War II sometime between the years of 1939 and August of 1945, and that this service remained a high point of her life in which she still took singular pride. Youth and serviceability reflected in the photograph, brought back memories of what she considered the good old days of her past.

It was both prying and tedious for me to observe her slow and meticulous execution of chores, such as removing her shoes and placing them toe to toe with the heels together and at right angles against the wall, and then pushing the length of her left hand down the length of the one leg of her nylons, grabbing a hold of the toe area and pulling the length of the leg up and out, and repeating this motion on the other leg to bring the nylons to the right side out. Watching her slow symphony of motions, I concluded that this woman was essentially a tidy and orderly woman, and this led me to the conclusion that her sister Evelyn must have been the one guilty of creating the outrageous clutter of objects over the entire floor of the dwelling quarters presenting a display resembling that of a gigantic garage sale. Largely due to Evelyn's miserly habits, the siblings dwelling quarters housed a collection of items both irrelevant and useless, and it was not surprising that I almost had my foot caught in a trap set for rats that was concealed under clutter.

Without a doubt, her oldest sister Evelyn, was the main culprit to have created an uninviting home atmosphere that turned aside many a suitor from the woman's door. This sister having given her life to the Lord at the tender age of nine, had made church-related activities her main priorities, and over the years, nurtured a resistance towards the attitudes popularly held concerning pursuits of fashion in dress, housekeeping and the acquisition of things material that would make household chores easier and less time-consuming. The McGuire sisters showed little or no regard for fashionable dress. Whereas Evelyn's two younger sisters, being less church-aligned, might have indulged titivation by adding a button or a bow to perk up a drab frock, Evelyn was completely void of a desire to partake in any such useless frivolity. Her dresses were homemade and basic: a neckline opening for her head to get through, two sleeves to free her arms for use, and a hemline that allowed her legs to stick out for walking. With serviceability uppermost in mind, her design and execution produced dresses that were mere unbecoming oversized T-shirts. To provoke disapproval from observers, she would wash clothing in a pan set under an outdoor tap, use a piece of wood for scrub board, abandoning the washing machine her brother had brought to the home to the invasion and occupation of rats and cockroaches. Any gadget that was modern, or any electrical appliance brought to the home, she would surreptitiously secrete under beds. Other peculiarities of her behavior included walking barefooted in public places and oiling her hair with coconut oil containing a touch of kerosene to ward off ants.

Over the many years the McGuires occupied the family home, they had achieved a certain position of respectability amongst the townsfolk, especially those who attended church, but on the other hand, they had put a jeering smile on the faces of those who knew of their eccentricities. Needless to say, this predicament would have proved a deterrent to keep young suitors away from the woman's door.

Her response to the routine of after-church chores shifted her actions into slow-motion in a house full of an eerie silence broken only by waves of heavy breathing coming from her brother and last surviving sibling. He was now stricken with cardiovascular complications that was failing to yield to the healing properties of the concocted brew utilizing the leaves of fifty bushes, notorious for its bitter taste and which was not working for him the way the ripe papaya poultices had worked to heal his sister Evelyn's bedsores.

Recollections of the pastor's proclamations on the afterlife were inevitably replaced by those of the timely deaths of her father, and later her mother, both in different rooms of the family home. She had only faint, childhood recollections of her bedridden, emaciated father coughing his life away with what she thought was a hole in the centre of his back, while her mother's cries of an excruciating pain, (believed to have been caused by cancer of the tongue, that had remained only partially responsive to morphine shots), were sometimes to echo from the ceiling of her death room. More vividly, and much later, the first of her three brothers, John, who springing up from his chair while holding his chest and crying out 'Oh my God!', died suddenly and unexpectedly from a massive heart attack on the verandah of the family home.

Reflections on the suddenness of John's death, invariably drew the similarity between his death and that of her sister Myrtle, who died surprisingly in her sleep from a stroke while on a visit to a foreign country. Complaining of a headache, she had excused herself to go upstairs to bed, and that was the last time she was seen alive. Though the passing of her second brother Cliff did not take place in the family home, but in the immediate neighborhood, it nevertheless took its customary toll on her emotions.

With six deaths in the home, that of Evelyn was to be the most draining on the woman's energies and emotions for the reason that she shared almost a lifetime with her in the family home, and was the main care giver over the six months that Evelyn remained unconscious on her back until she passed away from the complications of a stroke.

The death of close ones is normally traumatic, particularly to the young, but with the passage of time and maturing, and increasing exposure to the occurrence of the event, the upsetting effects death brings to one, usually diminish by varying degrees depending on the nature of the subject. For this woman, there was no room left in her heart for mourning, until her third brother, Peter, folded to the floor after his chronic health condition had deteriorated into a critical bout and he had gradually regained a remission which left him feeling on top of it all.

He arose that ill-fated Sunday morning with a hymn on his lips, and for the sake of olden times, he would polish and shine his black patent leather shoes to a mirrorlike shine as he had always done in preparation for church. He proceeded to partake of breakfast in the absence of his sister who was away at the time he began choking on his coffee. She had left to attend to the urgent matter of a faulty latch which was allowing the chickens to fly from their coop, when a helper solicited her assistance to save Peter who was now gasping for breath. The woman was not stirred to response having turned a deaf ear to her brother's emergency. She only shouted out repeatedly 'Can't you see I'm busy,' much to the bewilderment of the helper who was at a loss for a course of appropriate action.

Peter, in the meanwhile, managed his last act of defiance by pulling himself upright to stand on both feet and shuffle his arched body to his bedroom door, against which he slid like a fluid that collected onto the floor into a dead body.

The woman came to behold her brother's collapse, to check for his missing pulse, and to give the second to last of the six siblings a ceremonial burial with the rightful share of grieving .With a hardened heart and the wisdom of her years of experience, she knew that his troubled breath was at last freed of its restless tides:

free to rise and expand unencumbered.

At this point, the glow the pastor's words on the afterlife had put on her face, and which I detected when I first saw her in the queue of churchgoers, returned with the memory of his words of assurance that the last breath would ascend upon a wind to enter through the pearly gates into life eternal. She had been brainwashed into believing, and took comfort in her belief, that all good Christians went to heaven after their deaths.

Surviving her parents, her three brothers and two sisters, the last of the children, being only two years younger than Peter, was often nudged to ponder her own mortality as she found herself alone in the ghostly emptiness of the family home. Her hardened heart, however, would tide her over the doldrums associated with the loss of her brother, and take her to a place where yearning underlay the waiting to recapture the promise that belonged to her youth, in the sense of the following poem:

>
> Her heart like hardened fossil fuel,
>   Concealing latent fire-power,
> Awaited an explosive hour:
> To recapture the promise that belonged to her youth, ——
>   Such as at dawn, once more, ——
> To caress the sunlight and the laughter of swaying evergreens,
> To yield to the force that awakens dreamers to dance with the earth.
> With a heart smoldering and long-suffering,
> She concealed the ebbing hope, eternally springing and undying.

Hong Kong by night - The Lee Theatre Plaza in Causeway Bay

On Visiting Hong Kong

Having grown accustomed to the perpetual green of the vegetation covering every mountain and valley of Vancouver, I must admit that it was the brown sparseness I spied through the window of the aircraft on touching down over Hong Kong that was my first impression. We, the arriving passengers, followed the flood of lights and trouble-free leads to the immigration authorities, passed by airport personnel attending to their duties robot-like, as I exited through questioning eyes and looks full of uncertainty as to what country I might have embarked. I erased any suspicion of my possible intent and further interrogation, by declaring that my country of origin was Canada.

So as not to explore a description of the monumental engineering feat achieved in the construction of the Hong Kong International Airport, Chek Lap Kok, and its spectacular sprawl, let it suffice to say, that the magnificence of the Tsing Ma bridge leading from it, served as an impressive gateway to the gossamery mist of pollution blurring vivid details of the scruffy hills and the intricate waterways of the South China Sea at their feet.

On the way home through the outskirts of the downtown core, stately pines and whispering cedars of North Vancouver fell one by one in front of my imagining eye and gave way, each in turn, to a high-rise building, and, I soon came to the realization of what might have been meant by the term 'concrete jungle'. No trees to cut off the sun's light from flooding the landscape, hold you within troughs of cooler air, nor cast their motionless shadows over the ground beneath their canopy: as would have been the case in Vancouver. On the contrary, wherever in Hong Kong a welcome tree, or cluster of them, was sighted, it appeared rather isolated, thus ornamental and decorative.

The route home from the airport to Sai Kung in its rural setting, was circuitous. A road map outlining the way taken would have presented to me a formidable study having the number of streets and turns taken, overwhelmingly abundant. I fell under the illusion that the driver might have been driving haphazardly and that had he made a wrong turn, the mistake would have proved troublesome with only tricky recourse for correction, even for one as experienced as himself.

The immediate effect on my visit to one of the larger shopping centers, such as those that make up the Fashion Triangle in the heart of Central, namely The Landmark, Prince's Building and Alexandra House, was one of marvel at the opulence that greeted and held me in its spell. Shopping centers connected by covered walkways and unobstructed circles presented the open ambience of the outdoors, enhanced by magnificent skylights and fountains, spacious glassy marble floors and spectacular, tinged glass windows, all beset by giant pots of flowers and green areas of manicured gardens reminiscent of the artificial, and not unlike colorfully decorated birthday cakes.

This grandiose style of construction seen in these shopping centers defies the general rule found on the outside of these buildings: it invites the shopper not only into opulence, but into spacious confines without the humidity, heat or noise of the outdoors.

The serious shopper would enter the excitement presented in the abundance as well as the variety, —- and not a few surprises, delights and bargains available in a gigantic bazaar. However, I was mainly a window-shopper drifting in a delirium on what appeared a different planet, only to return to earth once I alighted onto the congested and bustling sidewalk outside the building. Not quite recovered from my delirious window-shopping experience, I allowed myself to be carried along the sidewalk by the human drift, narrowly escaping impact with double-decker buses and honking taxicabs. Buildings of shiny glass walls lifted my head to their impressive heights where I caught a glimpse of Mickey celebrating his seventy fifth year of unprecedented mousey glory within the magical world of Disney, as he wove unrestricted through the peerless illumination of the urban legends that belonged to the night and the city centre.

The kaleidoscopic effect of lights must set some measure for the brilliance by which all other city lights are to be judged. I was bedazzled by the neon lights of the downtown core which I can best liken to a colorful and brightly-lit Christmas tree of unrealistic proportions encompassing the reflections seen on the water of the Victoria Harbour, which divides the city into two spectacular portions. Caught up

A Hodgepodge of Reflections

in neon signs and the nightly congestion of human and vehicular traffic moving at snail's pace along Nathan Street, we browsed into the many shops and shot the breeze in awe of the throng of people, not unlike the scattering of spectators from a football game or rock concert.

On entering the wide expanse of a MTR station, I adopted a rebellious attitude and refused to run to catch the train unlike the crush of runners over-passing me while they hurried as though they were all late for the last train of the day. On exiting the station through the corridor, I momentarily became concerned that I might have been walking in the wrong direction, since everyone was coming toward me, so, I instinctively spun on my heals to face the opposite direction, only to observe that as many people were going my way. This phenomenon of overcrowding was new to me, but I soon devised a method for getting from point A to B through a moving crowd without making body contact. This was to slam through the crowd as quickly as possible with eyes cast to the floor in search of a clear spot ahead of me on which to plant my next step. Invariably this resulted in crisscrossing the floor without making eye contact with my competitor for space, or wearing a friendly countenance upon my face.

Not all of Hong Kong is renowned for its buildings of towering heights and bright lights, however. Leaving the glow of skyscrapers and the dazzle of reflecting glass walls at the city's skyline, we ventured out into unsophisticated sections, where "Hello Kitty" was to be found closer to earth in her intricate web of alleyways defined by painted walls checkered with grime and dust. Here was to be found the wee shops, each specializing in wares specific, such as you would expect to find at the Pen' Paper or the Rainbow Candy and Gift shops, that would entice you to enter their long and narrow aisles along which the shopper must work his way heedfully so as not to bump into the goods nor knock them from their shelves with his body. Room to move about freely is at a premium in Hong Kong, and this is so because the country has a relatively small living space for its population, thus the building code is based on the principle of maximizing living space by making it smaller for each person.

A good question to ask at this point is whether a barrel of salted peanuts in the shell, or one of dry shrimps, all look familiar after you've seen countless numbers of them one after the other set out to the front of the shops that line a street. One thing I found fascinating, was to observe the many unusual species of living creatures brought up from the deep blue of the South China Sea by exploitative fisheries, as they move in troughs set out on the sidewalk just outside a restaurant, and from which a customer could make his selection and have it cooked and served on an outdoor table by the sea. This is as novel as dining got in an unsophisticated setting.

Around every corner was to be spotted a well-attended eating place where dining seemed a happy occasion celebrated with enthusiasm and relish. "Eat, drink and be merry for tomorrow you may die", seemed not only a motto, but an attitude of the people. I soon learned that the people of Hong Kong had had a longstanding love affair with food, and that the country was recognized as a gourmet paradise of the latest, fine international tastes. Malaysian curry, or Indian naan bread, to give only two examples, could be the best in the world, as was to be found at Coco's restaurant in the fashionable Lan Kwai Fong.

Lan Kwai Fong is a rendezvous onto itself, standing unique and supreme as the nightspot of all Hong Kong. Here, we climbed up one of its steep and narrow streets, decided to patronize one of its string of pubs that, like many ahead of it, had only standing room on the sidewalk. Standing and drinking on a sidewalk lined with bibbers stretching as far as the eye could see in both directions, seemed incredibly exotic. It was definitely something that took me out of the ordinary. Having had drinks, we forged through the crowd up the narrow steep to the shortcut we took that ascending a rocky slope, arrived at a plateau where we encountered an overrun of emaciated stray cats inhabiting the dingy roofs below, and then descended some treacherous steps to a partially enclosed open air area with noisy diners, which was Coco's Malaysian Restaurant. The area was partially hemmed in by the walls of buildings that presented crude, white-washed surfaces made untidy by exposed piping and intrusive overhanging air conditioners.

The juxtaposition posed by this Third World atmosphere of my surroundings, set in the midst of an abundantly modern city, awakened the sleeping child within me to the magic of the night, and with freed spirit, I giggled mischievously at nonsense as children sometimes do. I could see from our depression through the opening above our heads, the tops of the swanky skyscrapers aglow in the night sky, presenting the striking contrast ever so adjacently.

Lan Kwai Fong was offering unique pleasures, and we sought to have an excess of it by yielding to the temptation to climb yet another flight of narrow and hewn steps that led up to the level of a pub with asymmetrical walls and floor space set under a tattered and sagging tarpaulin serving as a roof. Though seats were available here, we chose to stand around so as not to relinquish the good feelings of carefreeness that standing so far had brought us. We were in control of the night still buzzing after midnight with the movement and light-hearted laughter of loiterers, and only weary bodies, sleepy eyes and aching feet would take us down the narrow streets to our separate ways home.

Observing a fast-moving people execute their duties with devotion and immunity to distraction, I concluded that Hong Kong achieved success as a nation through devotion to industry, and that this good fortune was achieved through hard work and dedication, with time only for duty or leisure, and never idleness.

The preoccupation of merchants with the value of their goods, invariably naming their price in response to questions asked regarding the property of the commodity, I will attribute to a gap in communication. And if their economy seemed hard driven by materialism, it is to be remembered that a high regard for things material, though an essential ingredient of growth and progress, does not exclude room for things spiritual. The extent to which this is valid lies in the balance.

My poem to HONG KONG:

Astir and bustling, she marched fiercely forward
To the throb and rhythm of fruitful activity
Under the decree of her legacy: that of strife for survival,
And having triumphed to her new glory,
She marches forward boldly with confidence
To the throb and rhythm of daring and enterprise.

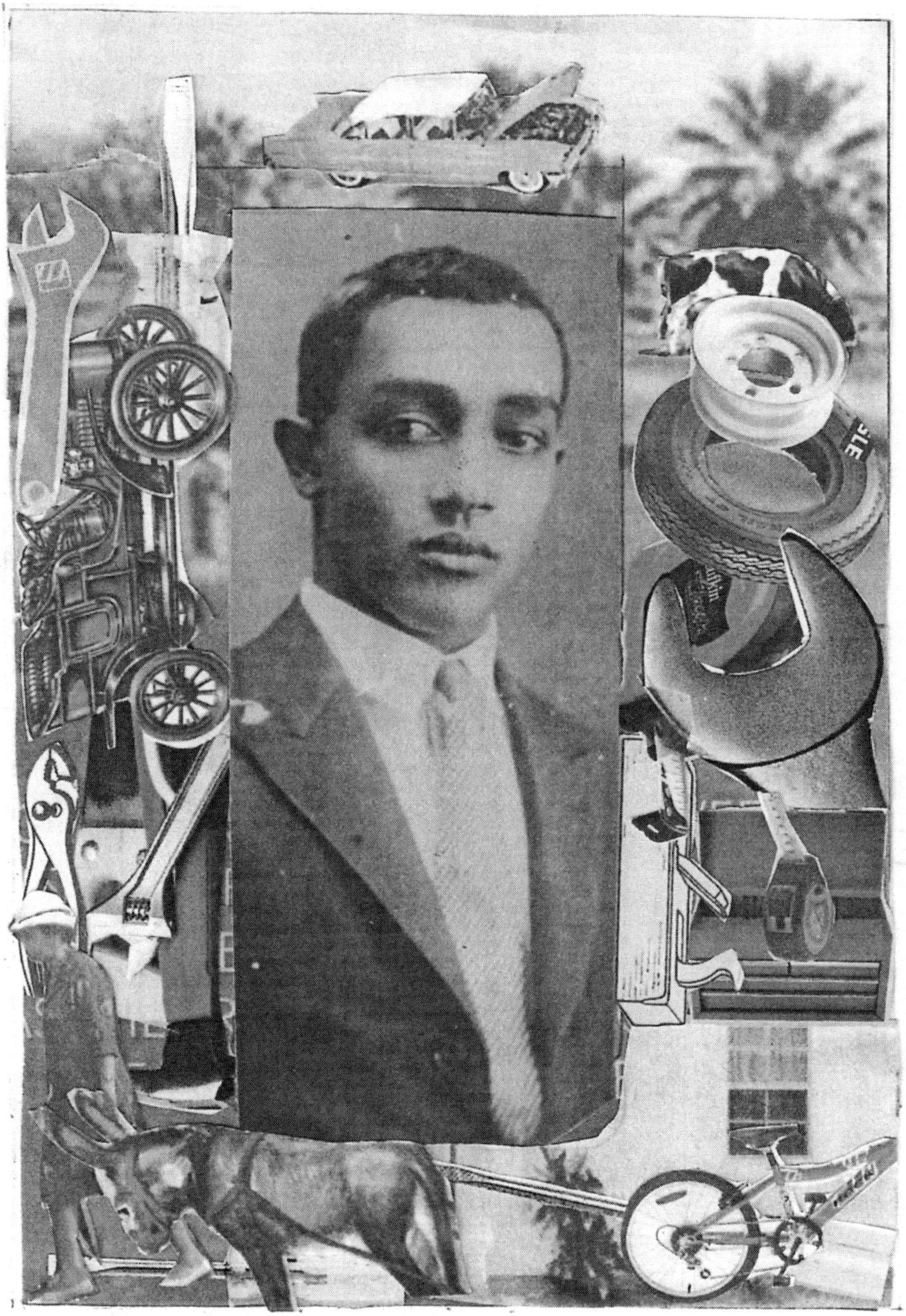

My Father

I knew a man I called Daddy, and who called me Miss Puss with a delight of great affection.

I knew a man who went to bed with the chickens, and who rose at the crack of dawn with the cocks to do a bit of crowing himself with an over-brimming surge of energy that came to him early in the day and spent itself in outbursts of song, recitation, or salutations, directed toward anyone within earshot. By late morning this energy depleted itself to leave Daddy fast asleep, open-mouthed from the last word, on a verandah chair overlooking the Caribbean. From which sleep he would awaken with a start, to pick up where he left off, while flipping his nostrils at the tip with an index finger, never forgetting to place his felt hat on his head in order to ward off an attack of sneezing or catching a cold.

It is still commonplace in Jamaica for children to be given pet names at some point of their lives. My father was no exception, and his first name of, Hubert, was soon shortened to Butty: the nickname by which he was widely identified and addressed, and which name sometimes hit a more affectionate note of Mass But, or the subservient tone of, Mister Mac. Only his personal and official documents such as passport or driver's license would have borne his proper name of Hubert Wesley McGregor.

Despite the old adage that 'early to bed and early to rise' makes one healthy, my father was to remain in poor health. He was resignedly accepting of his poor health, making only negligible effort to seek ways to improve his lot, even though this end would have been his first desire. This resignation came not only from his personal psyche, but from his time and place. His was the time when the word of the doctor, and the drugs he prescribed, were considered divine. Needless to say, he was not of a robust constitution, a condition he had not only grown accepting of, but that he used to gain sympathy from all who would lend an ear to his tales of woe. The truth is, the poor man had his first asthma attack at birth, and the last on dying, and on all the days between these two events. His heart and lungs grew weakened from too much asthma, and failed to sustain his life beyond the age of seventy two.

His life was a portrayal of contradictions. He was undoubtedly a man of the finest spirited soul that found himself in a body that emitted a comparatively dull aura which he endeavored to camouflage under a guise of vocal colorfulness. His friendly vociferousness drew a good many admirers, —— or should we call them well-met fellows, that liked him superficially with reserve, but never with a serious intent, or anything that could have grown into devotion. Too preoccupied was he with his health to fathom the depths of relationships, including those with wives and children alike.

My father was a cheerful sort, at least on the exterior, who kept his personal encounters on a light and jovial note by displaying aliveness to the precious ingredient of the moment, often expressing childlike astonishment in response to particulars. Always buoyant and playful with a disarming kind of charm, you would least have suspected that his outward display served to protect him from the anxiety of deep commitment. His jovial, well-spoken personality, coupled with his good looks and sex appeal, would win him the admiration of the ladies. But that is as far as that would go, since his overture at best, was pure flirtation on his part that would end with the social event.

He was an uncomplicated man who could not have played the faker for either love or money. At this point you may want to wonder whether his low physical stamina warded off the likelihood of his creating agendas stemming from ulterior motives. And so he lived from day to day, not as if it were his last, but with the hope for better tomorrows. Let it be said that in his own way, he held a number of people dear to him, including his children and grandchildren, and was even known to have doted on my daughter when in her childhood she became the object of his great pride and joy, and I know without a doubt, he felt her every pain as well.

A man afraid of his own shadow, was plagued by nightmares manifested by utterances coming from the grip of a terrifying experience, to result in a rude awakening —— a circumstance indicating a troubled nervous system —— avoided confrontation on all fronts, and always took the least line of resistance. I venture to say, he might not have been able to speak in defense of his own life, much less, collect that which was payable to him. It even proved difficult for him to scold his children out of fear they might create a scene that would bring tears to his eyes. This fear of confrontation, often mistaken for soft-heartedness, was a characteristic that seldom worked in his favor, since it was often interpreted as a sign of weakness. Ever so seldom, however, Daddy would vent pent-up anger in an explosive vocal outburst, never physical, for that he wasn't. Unfair criticism for something he had tried his best to accomplish with an aim to please, was something that would trigger such a release of anger. It stands to reason why he would have been wary of undertaking uncertain assignments out of fear he might undersell his capabilities.

As was the order of the day, self-employment that dabbled into this and into that activity, provided his livelihood. It was not strange, however, that he blossomed into an accomplished carpenter and the proud builder of houses, churches, and even a bridge, never having received a lesson on how to drive a nail, for he could only have been described as a prodigy of the art of carpentry. He was an ardent admirer of all things beautiful, finding particular delight in observing architecture in all its glory, and could be found peering into ceilings and at walls in search of symmetry in rafters, pillows and posts. He was a fixer of things around the house, and to a lesser degree inside the automobile, especially if a hammer and a piece of wood were needed to get the job done. This talent went with his capable hands that were elementary in form with thick square palms and short somewhat stubby fingers. Unfortunately his natural industriousness was limited to the wakeful hours of a frequent sleepyhead.

To gain the respect of the community and to do what was personally right by God, one was expected to attend church during my father's days. Sunday was a big day for church and for Daddy, that began at home with much preparation, including the weekly and lengthy tub bath, shoe-shining and dressing in Sunday-best clothes for attending either or both the morning and the evening church services. My father would return from church with song on his lips and the gift of tongues, regurgitating gilded words eloquently delivered by the Reverend Swaby from the Presbyterian church, while his sisters who never attended to have their fill of sermon, but for the sake of righteousness and out of habit, went to the Methodist church. Daddy had long broken away from the family tradition of Methodism to become a sermon taster of well-chosen pastors, regardless of their religious affiliation.

You might have recognized in my father a love for words and how they could be used to portray images and express ideas. No wonder my father took singular delight in quoting from Shakespeare and other writers, rattling off Latin declensions, theorems of geometry, and laws of physics that came from his treasure chest of high-school memories. Bursting into hymn or verse came suddenly, was sometimes used to deride or to approve a situation, but never as a surprise to those who knew him well.

Today I can look back with the understanding that comes with maturity, give reasonable reasons in defense of my father's behavior and the part he played in my childhood. The memory of the role my father played in my childhood is compounded by our mutual love and admiration and the knowledge that he was, to some extent, responsible for some of my emotional shortcomings which underlay much of my childhood unhappiness and underachievement in certain areas. He showed little interest in my childhood undertakings, and at best played the part of observer rather than participant, yet, he never failed to show elation whenever I did well, and sorrow at my failed efforts. If only he were less wrapped up in concerns about his health, how he might have found the will to foster and encourage ambition in those close to him and possibly influenced their lives in substantial and memorable ways!

The following poem encapsulates my concepts:

What of dreams that ne'er came my way,
    And of those that did, but finding no wings to boldly venture
        with the surge and urge of flight,
Halted within me, earth-bound and dull,
    Only to perish within a stunted soul !

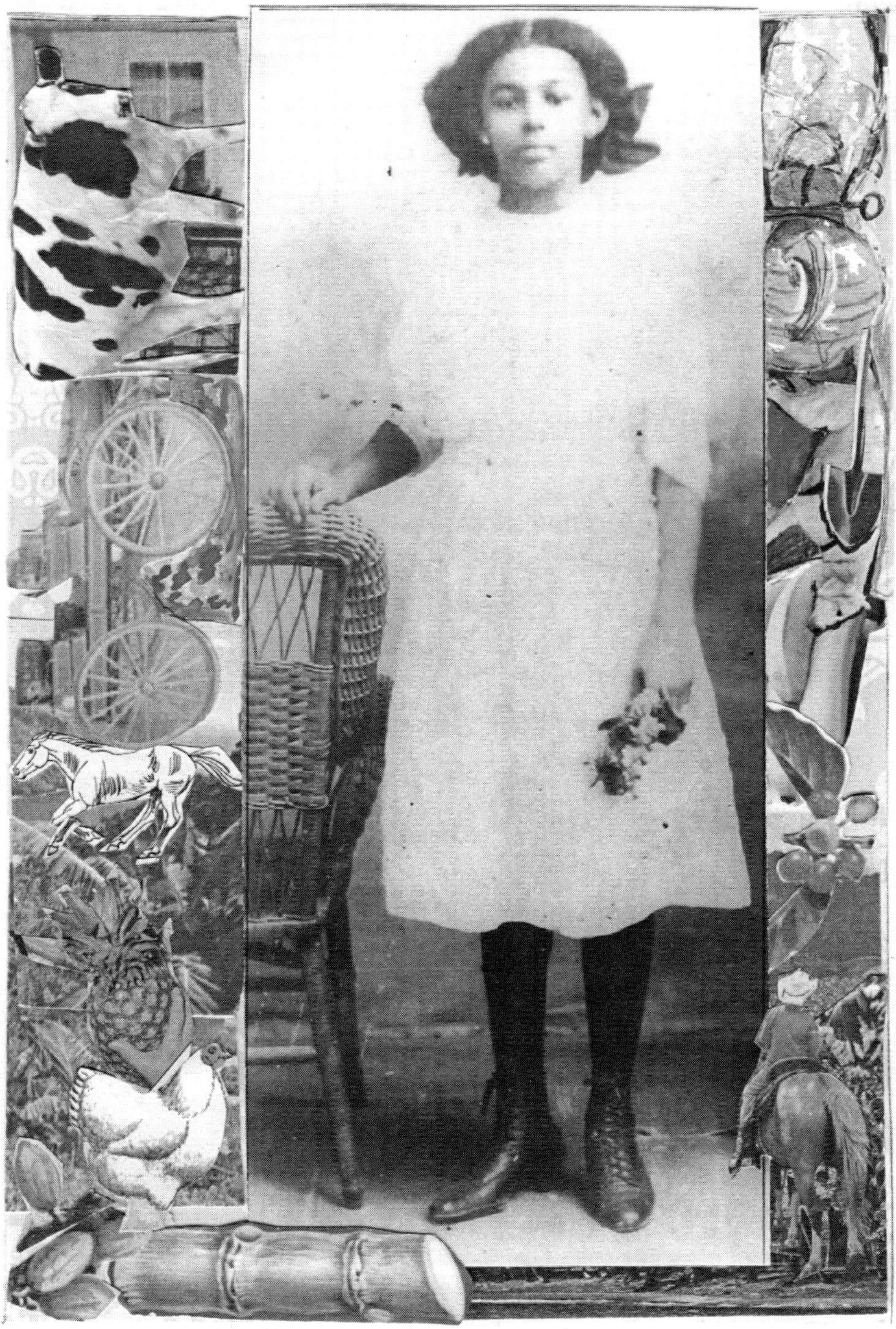

My Mother

To highlight the unfortunate events that occurred in my mother's relatively short life, is to paint a picture of misfortune. Her short story will somehow not give account of the happy times filling in between the milestones of her life.

As a young woman she married and eventually gave birth to a girl and later a boy, Mavis and Roy Magnus respectively, who both after relatively short lives, died battling epilepsy and mental deficiency. She was on her own, and there was no one to share the pain of a mother who thought she had done everything right during the pregnancies to have healthy babies.

Her desire to have a normal child and dissolve her marriage to her then estranged husband was strong, so she yielded to the wooing of my father, coupled with him and later gave birth to me while she was still married to her sick children's father. She later married my father after which my brother Derek was born almost six years my junior.

My mother and father, though married, were not soul mates. Often it seemed they never walked along parallel paths, especially the one leading to the garden in which my mother spent endless hours toiling with bare hands in the soil, to eventually produce a place of beauty. Not that my father was blind to the beauty of rose gardens, but that he found it difficult to show appreciation for her undertaking because of her wrangling him into appreciation, if not admiration, of her efforts. Without a doubt, there was an undercurrent of struggle between them, and this to me is one clear example of his rebellion against, what he might have thought, her cantankerous nature.

Echoes of her constant complaining about my father's shortcomings as a husband and provider reverberate in my brain. Nearly always these complaints were made in his absence, and nearly always I had no choice but to endure them as an unwilling hostage at her bidding. I do believe my father was negligent in certain areas of wedlock, but I cannot admire her response to his failure, because it was too immediate and volatile.

For though my mother was of a strong physical constitution and will, the condition of her nervous system displayed signs of frailty. Her neurosis resulted in compulsive acts and physical complaints without objective evidence of disease, and played a large role in her personality. She could be overly punitive and bad tempered, losing her cool collectedness, sometimes resorting to verbal abuse and derision, and was often found involved in someone else's fight. She once overheard my referring to her as a 'miserable being' in reaction to one of her outbursts of rage against me, and banished me to the proverbial doghouse where I was made to sleep on bare springs for about three weeks. I have always considered the severity of that punishment inappropriate for the offence. She must have had little or no idea of how irritating it was for a thirteen-year-old to be cornered, out of the clear blue, for an unwarranted lecture on how to be on the lookout for those occurrences in life that are beset by lurking traps of evil, when all I wanted was to be set free to learn about life from my own experiences.

I did not understand the intent of her prying and questioning into my every move, thus, they served only as a veil that came between my innocence and my self-esteem. Small wonder I could have perceived my mother as being less than calming to my sensitivities. To put it bluntly, as a child I always mistook my mother's crossness toward me for a lack of affection. Today, I reason it was only an element of her temperament, and that on some hidden level, her misinterpreted crossness came from caring.

On the other hand, I have always silently reflected on the occasion on which my mother asked me to sing her a certain song, and how the thought of her thinking I might have had a good voice warmed my heart; and the fact that she often harassed me to pick out her grey hairs with tweezers for a penny a piece, and how these two incidents, though today relatively insignificant, still serve as threads by which I hang to my mother's affection for me.

My mother was basically a most generous and kindly woman concerning things material: qualities that attracted and kept good friends who became strong allies. She gave of her belongings to the needy and the hungry, and of her time, to volunteer service in the Four-H Club, instructing young women in the art of cooking, especially in the making of peppermint candy canes, and guava jam and jelly.

A Hodgepodge of Reflections

Her impeccable taste in home furnishings, dress, entertaining and food won her the admiration of her associates. Despite the more popular music around, she chose to listen to Viennese-waltz recordings as they skipped beat over scratches on the over-used records she played on the wind-up Gramophone. Her preference for this music would not have been considered odd at that time and place, only a bit highbrow perhaps, nevertheless, in my mother's case, not false. Her efforts to awaken a sense of beauty and harmony in her physical surroundings drew energy from the moods and feelings of others and from the atmosphere of places and events, with seismographic precision. She strove to be aesthetically attractive and was characterized by her sense of modernity and of the beautiful. Her forthrightness in expressing her opinions, of which she was never in short supply, won her a reputation.

Jamaica was a colony of England during my mother's lifetime, and certain aspects of the English lifestyle had spread throughout the island. The English term 'high tea' came directly from this era and carried with it a certain unmistakable connotation of fastidiousness regarding style and fashion. Such attitudes were infectious, and the Jamaican middle class in particular, was absolutely infected by direct contact, as well as by the slower process of osmosis. Jamaicans were on a path of righteousness when it came to the execution of certain exercises such as preparing food and entertaining, among other activities. My mother and her seven siblings were no exceptions, being at least always conscious of the details to protocol. My mother saw to it that her children practiced the finer points of good table manners. She insisted that after a meal the knife and fork had to be closed straight across the middle of the plate in the direction one normally uses them. During meals we were not allowed to rest our elbows on the dining table, nor to slurp our food, nor to point with the fork or the knife, neither while making a point of view nor indicating direction. A soupspoon had to be filled with soup in the manner of pushing the spoon away from the body with the soup bowl slightly tilted in that direction, and the soupspoon lifted to meet the upright mouth along its long edge. Today, I am thankful to my mother that these practices she maintained have become habits of mine that have, on a personal level, served me well over the years. I consider drill a part of discipline, and discipline fundamental to most of life's successful undertakings.

My mother was a gifted cook, and a description of how she would have proceeded to bake a cake, serves to demonstrate colonial attitudes towards details. In my mother's house there was no electricity, so all cake-making procedures were carried out by hand-operated utensils instead of electrical appliances.

Eggs were cracked deftly, not only to avoid spillage, but more importantly, to avoid contamination of the white by the yolk. The catastrophe of contamination of the white would have prevented it from becoming stiff upon beating. A beaten white had to pass the stiffness test by being able to hang free at the edge of a hoisted beater and not fall from it. Only then would enough air have been entrapped to ensure maximum lightness of the batter and its end product. A mixture of the best butter and white sugar, carefully measured out, was creamed to a fluffy texture by stirring exhaustingly in a clockwise direction only, in order to enfold air. To this mixture, the yolks were enfolded one at a time with the same mixing technique. The sifted flour set aside with its full quota of air, greased, lined and floured baking pans, and the preheated oven to the desired temperature, awaited their turn to play their role in this painstaking, orderly undertaking. Once the carefully poured batter was added to the baking pan, the pan had to be lifted gently onto the oven rack, where it rested prominently as a labor of love. Then came the time of tiptoeing about the room so as not to disturb the cake as one waited nervously to glance at it from time to time to make sure it was rising and coloring nicely. Thinking the cake might be baked, it was gently pierced through at the centre with a pointed object such as a toothpick. If the object came up clean, this would indicate that the cake was baked. Needless to say, a perfect cake, worthy of praise and admiration, would have brought a sense of accomplishment to mother.

In my mother's time between 1900 and 1950, nearly all married women normally remained out of the work force to take care of the affairs of the home and their children. My mother, however, was not content in this role and always spoke of finding a job outside of the home or getting into some small business of her own. Her entrepreneurial spirit was ever aglow. Or was it that to her, longing was more important than having, and the possession of the object of her desire might have proved disappointing. She apparently could not live in the present which she might have found full of ordinariness. Perhaps if her longing was realized, it would not have been as special as the fantasy itself. With the undercurrent of wanting something other than what she was presently occupied with, she could not have remained still, because she was, and could only have been described as, a restless doer and a stirrer. Thus she found herself in the popularly acceptable occupation, even for a woman, of planting cash crops.

My mother was an extraordinary lady planter, challenging any man that dared to put his best foot forward in the cultivation of farm crops. Her field was a tropical mix of banana, plantain, yam, sweet potato, cassava, and taro to name the main crops. Not infrequently, and always without much ado or organization, she earned money from the sale of food produce to some casual buyer that came her way. Simultaneously, she turned her hand at raising a few chickens, pigs, cows, and goats in order to provide eggs, milk and meat for the home or for sale. Among farmyard helpers, were to be found, a donkey for riding, a mule for hauling and an occasional horse to pull the buggy for visits to her sister Doris. The farm was a bustle of activity, where my mother was the hard-working chief of operations from early o'clock till shortly after dusk.

A Hodgepodge of Reflections

She was a hardy woman who incessantly worked herself to a frazzle, and the things she could not accomplish standing due to her weakening stamina, she would do sitting, such as peeling cassava to make starch for sale, or kneading a leg of pork in its pickling fluid to make ham: two of her endless circle of chores. But mother was not well, and was making concerned visits to doctors who were not giving answers to her troubled state of health. Pills to ease the pain, and tonics to strengthen the bones, defined the nature of the treatment she received.

Father was not well with asthma in the room to one side of the dining room, and mother was not well in the room on the other side of the dining room, and I was not happy in the room between them both.

It was at Westwood High boarding school where I received a letter from my father reporting that Dr. Harry had done exploratory surgery into mother's abdomen and had sewn her up, for the spread of cancer he had found there was too far advanced for them to do anything about by way of a successful treatment.

My mother was so very alone at this time. She was her own care giver and counsel, but with the fortitude of a lion she found the strength to handle her problems. I remember her taking the country bus all by herself into the Linstead Hospital some three hours away to have the water drawn from her abdomen. Yet she was up and doing if the abdomen was not too extended. So with the passage of a year or so, Wilhel Lillian McGregor (nee Silvera), took to bed for a very long year or so, and eventually died as skin and bones at the tender age of 50 years, spanning the years 1900 to 1950. Her life program of that eternal quest for the Holy Grail ended without her realizing her dreams of getting into the work force or opening that small business nor seeing her children grow up into adults.

She left me the saddest girl in the world. Watching an ant crawl up a vertical wall on its errand, I envied it in it's happiness.

My poem dedicated to Mama follows:

Cut down in the prime of her life,
        to the level of death,
Death relieved her of earthly strife
        and found her a resting place,
Crowned her earthly head with laurels,
        like it did kings before her,
For she had triumphed over life
        having died.

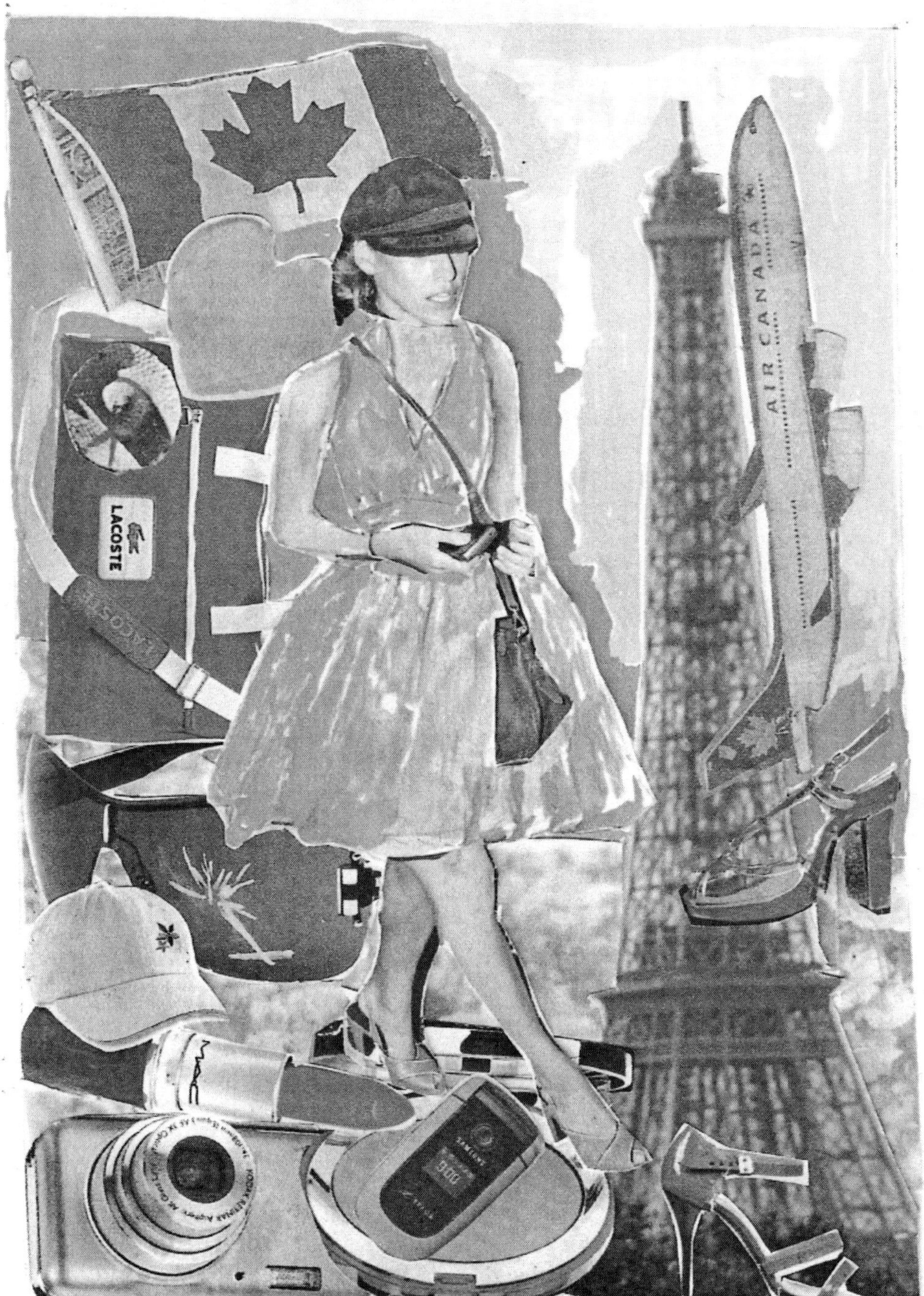

LACOSTE
AIR CANADA

Sarah Comes Full Circle

A best friend in Amanda was as good as life got for Sarah. Sarah was a well-adjusted eight-year-old girl with a happy disposition and a best friend to whom she was devoted.

Her day was complete whenever she had a good play with Amanda under the protective spread of the old apple tree in the backyard of the modest, middle-class home in which she lived with her doting parents and younger brother. At the close of day she could get her homework done, go to bed with a smiling face knowing that tomorrow Amanda would play the leading role in her day.

They would normally meet at recess time to play hopscotch on the pavement behind the school and share snacks and giggles at nonsense. The girls who could not get enough of each other, could hardly wait to share lunchtime and gossiping about the boys and girls wearing 'uncool' outfits, and those, in their opinion, committing weird acts. Among them were the favorites who could do no wrong in their eyes, and, on the other hand, there were the few who could do nothing that made sense. On weekends, the girls, like long-separated lovers, would spend hours on end talking on the telephone and bubble with delight whenever a 'sleepover' was permitted.

Sarah had always hated Paul Riley and his freckled face, and the ever chirpy way he responded to his teachers, always replying with full agreement without hint of back-talk. For her, he existed like the desk at which he sat, always there, inanimate and distant. Over the years the class moved up through the grades to the sixth, and though Paul had not lost his freckles, his responses had grown less irritating to Sarah, and more importantly, she began to notice that he had grown tall and lanky, and that his hair, ... she had no memory of ever having noticed before, ... was now fashionably spiked and somewhat attractive, ... though not by much.

As though Paul was guilty of making intrusion into Sarah's consciousness as being worthy of note, she now resented him in a new way, and must let him know it vocally. For the first time they were on speaking terms whenever she could muster words of contradiction or derision.

By the time she was twelve, her indifference towards the boys she had passed up through the grades with, had diminished; and also, they might no longer have been sharing the same classroom, and therefore, not only would have been out of sight, but out of mind as well. Sarah was still head over heals preoccupied with her many girl friends, though increasingly their gatherings often included boys that were taking on more human-like faces even though still charlatanistic to them.

Sarah and Amanda turned thirteen, and over the years, a good many new friends on both sides had slipped in and out of the girls' circle of friends. Amanda at the age of eleven, had moved with her parents to Hong Kong where her father had procured a job with Cathay Pacific Airways after having lost his position with Air Canada. The girls vouched to remain in touch over the miles of separation, and to visit each other should the opportunity arise. But with the passage of two years, the correspondence between them dwindled, and eventually petered out into nothingness. Wendy who sat beside her at choir practice had become one of a number of new friends taking over where Amanda left off, but on a different level of maturity. The quality of closeness she shared with Amanda would remain unique to the level of maturity the girls had attained during their years of friendship, and thus unrepeatable with any subsequent friend. In every true friendship one finds an answer to one's needs.

Sarah loved helping her mother in the kitchen as well as with the shopping for grocery and clothing, especially if she was allowed to choose a few items to her liking. Once in swift pursuit of her mother hurrying about the aisles of Zellers department store, Sarah skirted around a stand of shoes strewn into an untidy pile by impatient shoppers who pick up and toss items back in passing, so she just barely caught a glimpse of a rather attractive pair of pink sandals with high heels. Sarah had never worn heels quite that high before, and it was then that she recalled how sexy they looked on Jennifer Lopez in the movie, Shall We Dance. She was not afraid to suggest to her mother that she would like to wear shoes like the ones she had just viewed, on her upcoming trip to France. France she had always heard, was a hub of fashion, and she was inspired to plan a most stunning outfit for the trip of a lifetime.

A Hodgepodge of Reflections

Even though maturing takes place imperceptibly over the years beginning at birth, it is convenient to use the age of sixteen as the point at which Sarah emerged into full-bloomed young womanhood: a turning point to manifest itself on this auspicious trip to Paris. Like beginners in the arena of mating, she dreamed of finding a true love, of marrying and having children and a family she could call her own, and though this ambition existed only in the realm of dreams, it was nevertheless, on her agenda for that very special part of her future.

Under the guardianship and charge of Wendy's parents, she would accompany her best friends Tania and Wendy on the well-planned trip that would take them that summer on an elegant barge on a storied river cruise. But first she must endure the anxiety that comes with the prospect of a first airplane flight and travel away from home to a foreign country. On the other hand, she was quite confident that with her natural beauty and all the diligence she had put into the selection of articles of clothing for the flight, that not much could happen to hinder her from looking absolutely ravishing.

All of five feet three inches, she stood as tall as herself, girlishly slender in a summery, Algo 'Marilyn' rose-colored dress and matching sandals. With the allure of queen Cleopatra, she floated down the aisle of the 747 jet, aboard Air Canada's flight 184, bound for Charles deGaulle Airport. Her wispy brunet hair, shiny and bouncy about her shoulders, she took her seat behind a young man's head that held the promise of an equally attractive face.

Sarah did not attribute the cozy feeling of romance that was slowly wrapping itself around her like a warm blanket, to the phenomenon of travel to faraway, exotic places that brings out the romance in one and leaves the mundane behind. She yielded without resistance to the spell under which she was falling, while on several levels of consciousness, she divided her attention to the novelty of her new surroundings, to the demands of her friends, and to the male stranger sitting in front of her with whom she had already made eye contact while he was standing in the aisle. Deep down within her, she knew she would actually try to avoid him, while at the same time, take a secret interest in him, wishing that he would show blatant signs of a mutual attraction. She was smart enough to realize that her ego had come strongly into play, but that no matter what the outcome, she would not allow it to cause one jot of emotional pain.

She did not see his face again until he looked back at them and smiled over a shoulder in response to Wendy's rather embarrassing guffaw, as they shuffled their way through the throng of disembarking passengers heading toward immigration. The fact that she was never to hear his voice addressed to her, she reflected, could have been a blessing in disguise. An exchange of words between two people is essential to building a relationship, and to be honest she had no real desire of actually exploring her feelings for this stranger. The whole affair will remain a learning experience of falling in love with love and recognizing it for what it was, all within the limits of clean fun and overriding common sense. The last sighting of him making his way out of the terminal building through a revolving exit door brought finality to this brief one-sided affair. Only for a fleeting moment did she endure the pangs of separation as though from a beloved. Sarah was to suffer only momentarily as she drew strength from the solid emotional foundation put in place by the excellent parenting she had received. She bounced back from her brief disappointment to her old self, like a cork to the top of water.

The afternoon glow and cosmopolitan buzz of modern civilization that belonged to Paris, embraced Sarah bewitchingly as she entered, as though in a dream, the pearly gates to the highest expectations of events Parisian and magical. For Sarah, not all the viewing of the grand boulevards, historic national monuments such as the Eiffel Tower, masterpieces of fine art displayed at the Louvre and the pristine parks of Paris, could collectively rival the singular pleasure she derived from shopping in the boutiques lining the Champs Elysees, or just hanging out at a sidewalk café that epitomized the magic of the city of love.

Early next morning after their arrival, Sarah and her companions visited the seven hundred-year-old Notre-Dame cathedral to find it already packed with tourists, and the tour guides telling of its remarkable history and wonderment. While eavesdropping on the English-speaking guide, she would light a candle with the attitude of lipping a prayer, allowing herself to be caught up in the magic of the moment and following the example set by others around her.

Without lasting interest in the wonders of the cathedral, the girls soon flew outside an open door like butterflies seeking the light of the outdoors, and were soon to ask directions to the nearby Ile St. Louis of a young man, who incidentally was going their way. The island was a place famous for inexpensive creperies. As good manners would prescribe, the girls introduced themselves to their direction guide, and discovered him to be Tino from Italy, posted on assignment to a department of men's fashions in Paris.

Under Tino's leadership, they squeezed through parked buses just behind the cathedral, crossed the busy street, and later entered the iron gate into the park at the tip of the island, descended the stairs that led to the Memorial de la Deportation. This memorial to the 200,000 French of the Nazi concentration camp, drew them into the experience of the victims who suffered there. The city around them was now out of view and the surrounding walls held them like prisoners whose only freedom was the view of the sky above and the glimpse of the river below.

By this time, Tino had already made impressive inroads into Sarah's admiration as she was to become mesmerized by his distinguished blend of physical appeal, captivating accent and charming manners, and above all, his savvy of things local and last but not least, his effervescent uninhibited ability at luring.

And though he was equally nice to all the girls, Sarah must have had her reasons to come to the conclusion that he was partial to her, and for that very reason he had invited them to dine at the Café-Med, and later to the jazz club, Le Cave du Franc Pinot. Surely, he could have taken off on his own after having shown the girls the island, but the fact that he made an effort to remain in their company was indication for Sarah that he was indeed attracted to her. Her feelings were bolstered when later at the café, he told her she was beautiful. She would cling to those words of flattery like a treasure she carried in secret next to her heart. She felt at this time he could have persuaded her to do something rash, and that was when on the dance floor he planted a kiss on her lips.

Once more Sarah was to be guided by reason. She was aware that the attraction to Tino, though real, was only superficial and that there would have been much more to explore and discover about one. Yet, for all the pleasure flirting brought, she wanted to see him again, perchance to get his address and the promise of a future when they could possibly meet face to face once more. His magnetism had pulled her towards him, to a place where she was losing control to resist the desire to meet with him again.

He was, as she would have liked, the perfect gentleman who walked them home to their hotel, the Grand Hotel Jeanne D'Arc at 3 rue de Jarente.

The day ended for Sarah on a perfect note with a standing arrangement that they should meet with Tino again at the jazz club in the next two days on Saturday, July 5th at seven o'clock in the evening. She had two days to fill with activities touristic while her brain bubbled with silent anticipation and a trace of apprehension of their rendezvous with Tino.

Saturday came, and the girls arrived at the club on time, looking like twinkling stars on a clear night. They procured seats for themselves and an extra chair for Tino which remained prominently vacant. They filled the long hours from seven to nine exchanging experiences on holidaying in France with two English girls visiting Paris like themselves, while they awaited Tino's arrival, … Sarah venturing mousily now and again through the clamorous crowd in search of a face that would be Tino's.

By nine o'clock the girls gave up any hope of his arriving, and decided to leave the club like hurt dogs carrying their tails tucked under. Disappointment dulled Sarah's countenance, but her coping mechanism came into play and she was not making excuses for Tino, but cushioning her personal disappointment with a new philosophy that became a part of Sarah's strength and new wisdom.

For the sake of a new experience, the girls decided to walk along pont St. Louis that connected the two islands, otherwise referred to as the pedestrian bridge, and later to take in the Latin Quarter for colorful wandering at its best. The neighborhood's touristic fame relates to its intriguing bohemian character, where the haunts of great poets and philosophers of yesteryear are today the hangouts of tired tourists.

Walking along boulevard St. Germain which provided a reprieve from the general squalor of the somewhat defunct Latin Quarter, they spotted in the distance what looked like an elegant lady walking a poodle, accompanied by a male figure. The lady would have been slight and clothed in dark colors, contrasting nicely with the white of the poodle and the light color of the male companion's outfit. More and more, as the two parties approached each other, the male figure began to look a lot like that of Tino. Sarah could not have endured a close encounter with Tino at this stage, so the girls decided to change direction to a side street and take shelter from view by hiding behind a lamppost from which position they could spy upon the threesome as they passed by. The girls sheepishly awaited the arrival of the strollers with bated breath, and later confirmed their suspicion that the male was indeed Tino. Several questions as to his relationship with the lady will remain unanswered. I daresay, that it would have been upsetting for Sarah to find out that the lady was romantically attached to Tino. Before the return trip to the hotel was completed, the girls were giggling about the whole episode, even though an empty light-heartedness overcame Sarah.

Sarah pondered the sequence of events of the time they spent with Tino, and saw how easy it could have been for an innocent girl to be caught in a web of deception and for her to delude herself into believing what she wanted to believe, or, on a deeper level, how the very survival of a relationship could depend on the telling of lies, whereas the telling of the truth could be detrimental. Sarah was making great strides in growing up to become a smart lady.

Sarah was to return home a bit older and wiser, and it showed in the way she wore her hair: scraped back into a sleek ponytail secured by an elegant red, silk-rose clasp to match her red jacket. If only she could have seen how lovely she looked, and how fortunate a girl she actually was with most of her life ahead of her within a homeland full of opportunities second to none. But Sarah was not reflecting on her good fortune, but on her immediate feelings of fatigue and post holiday blues.

With long black lashes resting on her petal-soft skin, and the characteristic slight pout to her full lips, she shuffled into the comfort of her seat under the dimmed cabin light of the aircraft, and slept like a baby. She did not do much else on the return flight, but briefly thought of how well she wanted to do in school in the upcoming year, and on a secondary level, did she imagine herself with a steady boyfriend with whom perhaps she would make love.

Her father was at the airport to meet her with a warm embrace into which she snuggled and felt the wealth of his paternal caring with its special quality of a teasing joviality. Never was a girl's love for her father felt so strongly as at that moment. Sarah was awake and happy to recapture the old feelings of the life she left behind for two short weeks. The experience of her trip to Paris was not to be put behind her, but in a very special place etched in her memory.

A Hodgepodge of Reflections

It was an auspicious occasion on September the fifth, 1979, when Sarah began the new school year at Windsor High School, because it was full of anticipation of good times with friends and the richness of an active social life which she quietly craved on the inside, despite her outwardly somewhat introverted personality. School, so far had posed less than average challenge to this academically gifted student who, without extraordinary effort had achieved an impressive record with only minor concerns on her part, regarding her lack of inclination to participate in athletics. Her scholastic success may be attributed to her native talents, as well as to concerned and loving parents who were dedicated to helping Sarah realize her highest potential.

On the very first day of school, Sarah learned that Judy from her circle of friends had received accolades for her distinguished performance of Liszt's Liebestraum No. 3 at a school piano recital, and that Janet was selected to play the leading lady in a church production of Everyman. The thought occurred to Sarah that though travel offered unique opportunities for widening ones horizons and gaining new experiences, it did cut one off from home-spun rewards.

Sarah was taken by surprise when on the first day of school she came face to face with Paul Riley while she was ascending the steps to the library and he was coming down in the opposite direction. They were alone in the stairwell, and the moment of meeting tinged with a certain irony and clandestineness, found Sarah caught up in an outpouring of enthusiastic greeting and chattiness, both deliberate and heartfelt, and she knew it was coming from a place of guilt and shame for the years over which she had harbored a loathing for Paul. She reflected momentarily on how she had changed in her regard toward the opposite sex since she was six, the age at which she first met Paul.

There was Judith, the new girl to the province and school from Quebec who took social studies in the same class as Sarah, and whom Sarah opted to take under her wings while she enfolded her into her circle of friends. This relationship, however, was mutually beneficial, since Judith got to learn about her new school and city through Sarah's guidance, and Sarah got to unfold her maternal instincts easing Judith into her new environment. Judith, is to become instrumental in bringing Sarah and her first real boyfriend together in the near future.

Out of appreciation for Sarah's extension of friendship and her all-around assistance in helping Judith to adjust to her new environment, Judith had Sarah over for a weekend that the girls were to spend at Harrison Hot Springs. On what could have been the hottest day of September, the girls would soon be splashing buoyantly in the enticing lake water. A good day would end with the girls dining at a restaurant of their choice selected at whim. By remote choice only, they spotted a fellow student amongst the diners at the restaurant. The tall blond and basketball star, Kevin Baker, greeted the girls on his way out of the restaurant and left them with jovial assurances that they would more than likely run into one another the following day.

Sarah had seldom seen Kevin since he was a year ahead of her at school where she knew of him only by the link of his name to the game at which he excelled. The prospects of further encounter with Kevin on this trip, left her with mixed feelings of indifference tinged by a bit of intrigue. The weekend had suddenly taken on a new and unimportant curiosity to banish all possibility of boredom.

Sarah felt something was missing from her day when by late afternoon the following day they had not met up with Kevin and his friends on the beach, around the town, nor at the restaurant where they had dined the night before. Sarah banished Kevin from her mind to the place he held in her consciousness before they met on this trip.

But sooner than you would have imagined, fate would bring both Sarah and Judith together with Kevin the very next Friday at a barbecue party at which all three were guests. Once again, Sarah was in attendance on Judith's invitation, as the party was hosted by Judith's mother's friend. Strangely enough, Kevin explained that he had looked out for the girls at the resort but failed to locate them, and this revelation served to mend any broken fence. The chitchat between them was casual and intermittent at best. The party crowd dwindled, and despite Sarah's admiration for Kevin's poise, quiet reserve and good looks, her feelings toward what she sensed as his ordinariness, failed to kindle amorous notions within her. He hung around long enough to brave what he faked to be a spur-of-the-moment invitation to the girls to watch him play in a friendly basketball game to take place that evening in the school's gymnasium. The girls, caught off guard, had no time to refuse the invitation and were soon to be witnessing Kevin score points in their estimation as well as on the court. Kevin's performance at the game that evening, elevated him from the average to the extraordinary, in Sarah's final assessment.

Sarah herself was driven to excel at whatever task she undertook, thus her admiration for Kevin's enthusiasm was natural. They had something in common, and this was to serve as the platform from which a friendship between them would be launched. It was not strange that the memory of Tino occurred to her at that moment, and how he had swept her off her feet into a whirlwind of fascination that ended abruptly with a degree of disappointment. Sarah was not about to dive again into deep waters of fascination with a virtual stranger without due caution. Perhaps the way to a lasting relationship is through friendship and the sharing of common interests.

Sarah was about to find out that Kevin fell short of her full admiration in matters non-athletic. Out from her bubbling lightheartedness, and without contemplation, Sarah blurted out a casual invitation to Kevin to her seventeenth birthday party, which was to take place the following Saturday in her backyard.

Kevin showed up to the party with a friend with whom he remained preoccupied, and made minimal effort to mingle with the other guests even though he had been properly introduced to them. Kevin's exclusivity and lack of partying know-how, did not go unnoticed by Sarah, and this was the first strike against him in the game of dating.

The partying teenagers were soon to retreat from the adults to huddle in Sarah's bedroom where they wound up playing the board game called Cranium. Sarah was embarrassed at how slowly Kevin caught on to the rules of the game even though it was new to him. With a calculated look across the table, she saw his weakness, felt her intellectual superiority, and reasoned that a relationship with him would probably work well to her advantage. She would be happy to use her maternal bent, to be his guiding light in matters social and cerebral, and he would provide in person, her handsome basketball star and lover. Sarah enjoyed the thought of having what she deemed the upper hand is this arrangement, regardless of its tenure. She was motivated to use this design as the basis of her entrapment of Kevin, realizing that the scheme came from her need to be needed. However, she thought it best to play the waiting game and allow the friendship they had established so far, to blossom, perchance, to become full-bloomed.

Sarah's wiles fully captivated Kevin with his full share of romantic thoughts, and the two were to become friends and lovers for a period of about four months. However, Kevin's shortcomings regarding the social graces and his lack of interest in matters thought-provoking, were to drive a wedge between the friends that would push them apart and cut at the strings of attachment.

The incident that severed the fraying connection happened when Sarah's doting grandmother Edna, wanting to meet Kevin, asked them both to accompany her to her sister's where she was to dine. Edna transported the youngsters to dinner by car in which she was carrying a fairly heavy box of food items. Both Edna and Sarah were disappointed in Kevin in that he allowed Edna to carry the box to the house without offering to help her. And to add insult to injury, he failed to thank Edna for the ride and invitation, and his host for dinner.

Sarah precipitated the breakup with Kevin by her repeated display of boredom and displeasure in his company, but wasted no time accelerating her encounters with girl friends in an effort to fill the new void created by the separation, and to cover up the little guilt she felt. She and Kevin drifted in opposite directions, but were to remain on friendly terms by mutual consent.

Sarah chose to remain out of the arena of intimate relationships for as long as it took her to execute celebrative preparations for the approaching Christmas season and to land a speaking role in the school production of Hello Dolly to be staged in the new year.

It was Sarah's ability to turn a tune to the satisfaction of the judges, to project her speaking voice across a crowded room, and the lessons she had received in ballet and hip hop, that earned her the part as Irene Molloy. Though on stage, she was the love object of Cornelius Hackl, it was his fellow stage employee, Barnaby Tucker, who in reality, had his eyes set on Sarah. Initially, Sarah's attraction to Brian was purely physical, but with the overdose of exposure to him resulting from hours of rehearsal together, she cautiously grew to like his jovial personality and keen sense of humor, often bringing amusement both on and off stage. This quality, common to Brian and her father, brought intrigue to play in Sarah's thoughts. The knowledge that her strong attraction to Brian was serious, and that she was unsure of the extent of his feelings toward her, posed some concern for Sarah. Sarah's feelings fed voraciously on Brian's flirtatiousness and she could hardly conceal them from him, and he being the boy he was, played right into her hands.

Sarah was beside herself with erotic feelings for Brian that rivaled those she felt for Tino: Recognizing at the same time that not only were they more clear-sightedly based, but that she was in a more opportune position to explore them. The relationship, however, did not grow from friendship, as was the case with Kevin, but started off at the deep end with sexual encounters. Sarah could not see enough of Brian, wanting to be constantly in his company, whereas, Brian showed a greater desire to hang out with his male companions than to spend time with Sarah. She took every opportunity to be present wherever Brian would be, especially at the practices of the band in which he was the guitarist. She even secretly became obsessed with the idea of taking singing lessons, perchance to sing with the band.

Sarah was astonished when she realized that she was capable of jealousy which she felt whenever Brian showed a preference to spending time with his cronies than with her. Brian, however, was not about to change his ways, and grew resentful of her clinging-vine behavior.

Sarah's feeling of insecurity in Brian's affections escalated into frustration which she could either have endured, or she could have chosen to sever the relationship. There was no easy solution to the problem facing Sarah. The devastation of a breakup was likely to have been initial and short-lived, whereas the tortures inflicted by Brian so far, had no end in sight. Sarah's pride took a front seat and drove her to the decision to sever the relationship with Brian: and that was what Sarah did for herself. Brian was mildly disappointed at Sarah's decision, but managed well to live with it. He was after all, genuinely fond of Sarah and wished her only the best, but he was only a boy with his own unique set of problems.

The affair between Sarah and Brian, could have led to the altar and become another occurrence of childhood sweethearts getting married, if it were balanced, having Brian's ardor being equal to Sarah's. Little would Sarah have been aware that she likely made the right choice, as her vision was limited to the present and clouded by a lack of fulfillment that was the product of her youth. She was not aware of the fact that the separation rate among teenage marriages was relatively high, due to the fact that the partners tend to diverge in separate directions along the path of maturing into ripened adults.

A Hodgepodge of Reflections

Sarah was wise beyond her years, and it was not surprising that she came to the decision to forgo romantic involvement with the opposite sex during the completion of her secondary and tertiary school years. She would become atypical amongst her peers by channeling her sexual energies into scholastic achievements. The experiences she gained from dating as a teenager would, nevertheless, be invaluable to her future involvement with men.

Steadfast to her resolve, Sarah completed her last year of high school with full participation in the academic as well as its social demands, to graduate with honors and a special reward for her overall high achievement. Well-being and a sense of accomplishment put Sarah in a frame of mind conducive to playing around with various options as to what undertaking she should pursue in the immediate future.

The approaching summer was open to days of play and fun in the sun, and the procuring of gainful employment was a natural command. But deep in her heart she cherished the wish to attend a university, preferably somewhere out of province, if not out of country.

Though she spent the summer of 1980 between two part-time jobs, as an usher at Storyum, and as an assistant in a Gastown gift shop, and even managed to squeeze in driving lessons with Young Drivers of Canada into her busy schedule, the main focus of her attention was getting together with her friends for leisure and pleasure.

That autumn, her wish came true when the University of Toronto accepted her to a course of studies that would gain her a Bachelor of Science degree majoring in chemistry. She figured that during this first course of studies she could determine more precisely the direction she wished to explore in the field of chemistry.

At university, Sarah grew to become less of a social butterfly while coping with the time-consuming and relatively rigorous demands of study. Here she made only a few new friends, and the effort to maintain the friendships she left behind in Vancouver was straining for survival, and she was aware that they would probably weaken with time and geographical separation. The people she socialized with in Toronto were mostly her relatives with whom she boarded. During her high school years, Sarah had, on an emotional level, detached herself from her relatives in a desperate pitch to establish her independence, but now that, that need was disappearing, to the extent that she no longer minded being seen attending a movie theatre with her grandmother, and even favored the company of relatives over that of friends.

Over the next two years she was relentless in the application of her new philosophy to stay out of the dating arena as a precaution against interference to her targeted academic aspirations.

It was her lab instructor who first tugged at her resolve with his attention to her needs and showers of compliments. His flattery brought her to the point where she found herself resisting making a comparison of her feelings for him with those she felt for amours of her past. Though compelling, it was nevertheless harmless, she reasoned, to really like Rodney Stuart and keep a level head about the association, and not allow it to upset her equilibrium nor break her resolve. Special friends only is what she deemed they would remain. But, as was her experience in the past, her feelings for Rodney, once fully reciprocated, grew into the monster to overpower her resolve and throw her into a ditty of sweet sourness. Sarah and Rodney were to become quite the couple on campus as they complemented each other quite nicely, so much so that Sarah hailed the union as mature and stable, and with such an attitude that enabled her to complete the school year to the grand climax of graduation.

Unfortunately, there was an undesirable development for Sarah in the works, despite all due precaution to avoid it. The surprising news that she was actually pregnant, struck an earth-shaking blow to her nurtured ambition to further her studies toward becoming a researcher in the field of medicine, and to her treasured wish to become pregnant only after marriage at an age in her early thirties. Rodney on the other hand, was older and more amenable to the prospect of marriage to Sarah and becoming a father. He, with great adoration for her, was able to console and encourage her into the acceptance of a shotgun wedding, never failing to promote the excellent prospects of her returning to complete her career dream.

Once she was able to project her vision of the future onto the completion of her career aspiration: nevertheless, with a beautiful baby girl sleeping quietly somewhere in the background, she was able to accept her marriage as a happy one. Rodney's goodness and devotion to Sarah, was her pillar of strength, and it was to be hoped that she did nothing to upset the applecart. Theirs was a match that had the markings of success about it, despite Sarah's deep-seated resentment toward marriage and baby all too early in her life.

Sarah suffered only briefly as a result of postnatal blues, but was mostly grateful for a beautiful and perfect baby girl who soon filled out in the cheeks to having a face all of her own and that no longer bore a striking resemblance to her aging grandmother. Sarah who was only partly thrilled with motherhood, was soon to be nagged by the pattern of drudgery it presented, and the deep desire to be free to pursue her ambition surfaced intermittently. On the other hand, the feeling of shame she felt to have entertained the option of having an abortion, was overcome by great relief that she had independently decided against it.

Beyond Sarah's wildest imagination, bonding with her new daughter Leah, was to bring an end to her struggle with motherhood and a discovery of the extent of love possible between mother and child.

A Hodgepodge of Reflections

Still apprehensive about what the future held in regards to fulfilling her career aspirations, she began to reason that it would be wise of her to return to her hometown in order to rally child-care support from her many relatives, thus allowing her more time to pursue her studies at a local university. This idea was soon dismissed when Rodney accepted the offer of a position, with almost unbelievably lucrative rewards, by the University of New York.

If you knew Sarah, you would not be surprised that the prospect of moving to New York city would be most exciting and acceptable to her in all its shining possibilities. And moreover, with all the money coming their way from Rodney's earnings they could certainly afford the services of a nanny of sorts. With a renewed sense of adventure, Sarah's spirits soared to new heights of expectations of what life may have in store for herself and her young family. To top it off, she was accepted by the University of New York where she could pursue her career ambitions. Without a fly in the ointment, she embarked on this new turn of her life in the sense of the following words:

Nurtured on the greening grass,
Sapling girl, thrived on guardian care and loving
Till her days of childhood passed —— like the polishing action of the waves upon pebbles ——
And she, like a gleaming stone, tossed onto the shores of a new wisdom,
Set her roots deep to pervade the browning grass,
And, like a cackling hen brooding over fertile eggs,
Stood tall to embark upon her new beginning.

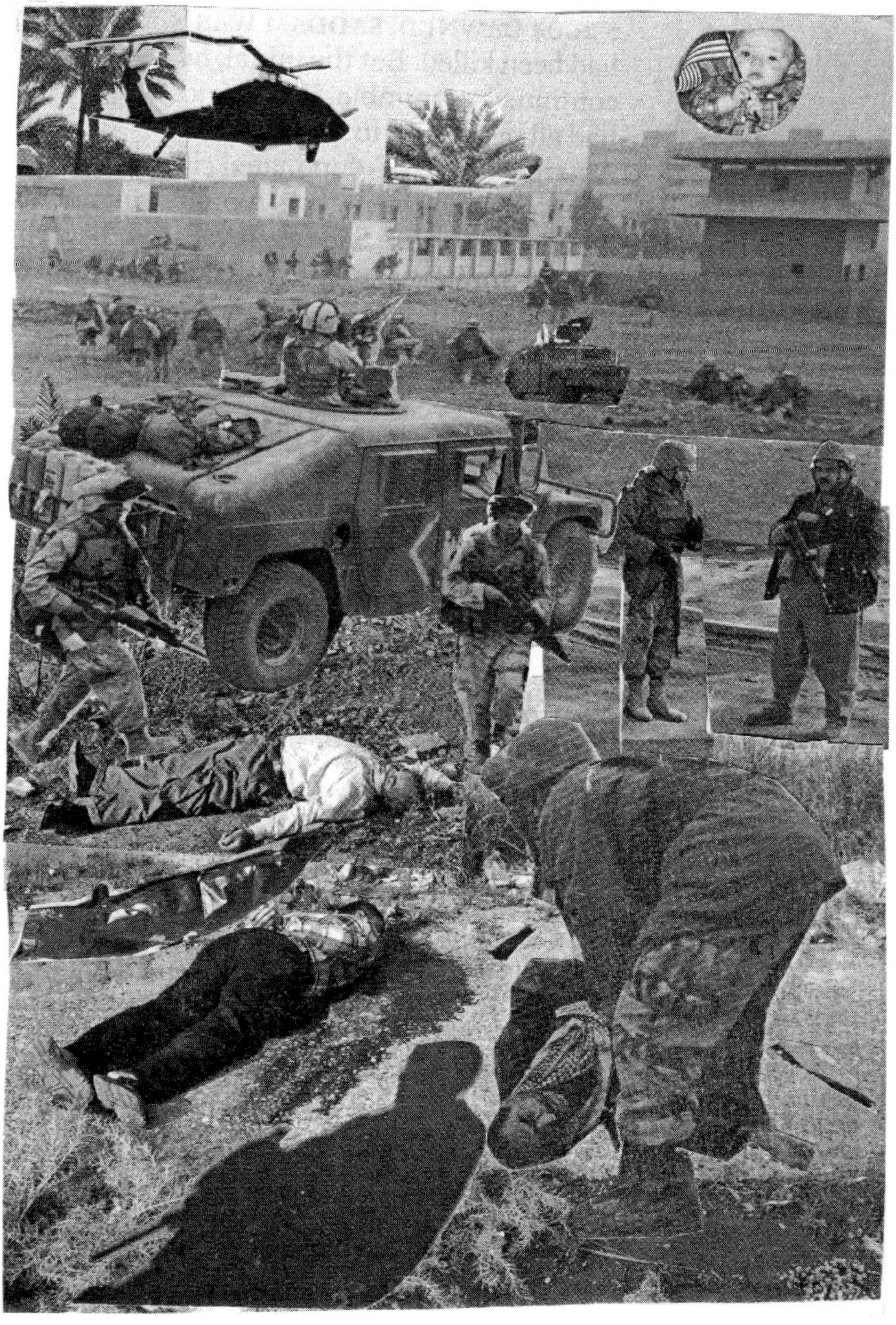

Disillusioned Soldier

His cry at his birth was strongly spirited and louder than his mother's howls of labor, and portended of a superior vitality, and all the potentials of this quality. The throes of birth had rushed his blood to his face to produce a cherry-colored glow beneath his black skin. Already his agonized face showed the age and wisdom of his grandfather to whom he was showing a striking facial resemblance. Beneath his infancy, he was already a man that had taken on life by the tail: for all the very many things that could have marred his birth, none was evident in this perfect child who seemed to be one hundred percent normal. As for his newborn facial features, they were only temporary, and would soon conform to the laws of nature and fill out with baby fat into normal babyhood, to be followed by normal boyhood and subsequent manhood —— he'd emerge as a man for all seasons.

So with a good physical start and the caring of devoted parents, Calvin Brown began his life on the fifth day of June in the year 1979, as the first child to a lower middle class family in the small Jamaican town of Ramble. His mother worked as a servant in the middle class household of a lawyer and his schoolmistress wife, while his father served as the headman who oversaw the workings of an orange plantation. Their combined incomes did not allow for the purchase of luxuries, but for this thrifty and stable couple, would do for the necessities of housing, food and clothing, and other healthful provisions for their son.

Calvin was to receive his elementary schooling at the local public school, and would attend the Baptist church along with his parents, who were devout Christians reading the Bible for its unquestionable truth and its ultimate guidance for the proper conduct of living.

His parents themselves, were not highly educated, completing only the elementary school grades. Thus his father, compensating for his personal deficit in scholastic achievement and unfulfilled dreams, tried to recoup and realize in his child, that which he himself was denied.

In his anxiety to enrole his son in the first grade at the age of six, he had had his wife put in an order for an ample supply of khaki uniforms, comprising of short pants and matching shirts, which were to be duly starched and pressed, some two years ahead of time. Every detail was perfected in the preparation for Calvin's first day of school, both in the physical, as well as in the emotional departments. The first weeks of light and playful introduction to the routine of school were soon to be followed by his teacher's drilling techniques, and his parents' nightly supervision of his homework. Everyone was pleased with Calvin's adjustment to school in general, as well as to the academic leaps he made in the three R's.

Up to the time Calvin entered the sixth grade, his father, familiarly called Mr. Buck, himself a perfectionist, had lived a life of dedication to duty, seriousness and responsibility, and had inadvertently imparted this idealism to his son. It was about at this time that Calvin began to internalize the demands of his father who, as it were, had taken up residence inside the boy. It would have been Calvin's own punishing voice that would accuse him whenever his behavior fell short of his father's expectations. The issue here, however, was not objective self-sacrifice or goodness, but what he considered to be such. Before the boy could begin to redeem himself, he must first recognize this internal state of conflict before he could begin to grapple with it in an effort to accepting himself as an okay guy without being perfect.However, Calvin was yet too young to recognize this dilemma that would only emerge in his future, having woven negative traits into his character. His would be the challenge to recognize his problem, before he could begin to work on a solution.

In the meantime, Calvin was bursting at the seams with internalized parental demands that were now shaping the code of his day-to-day conduct. He had reached the point in his relatively short life, where he was denying his natural inclinations to play or to enjoy leisure pursuits, choosing to perform instead, tasks he deemed dutiful. No longer in the mornings did his mother have a problem getting him out of bed to prepare himself for school, as he kept growing more conscious of duty and responsibility. He was showing early signs of compulsive punctuality. Whenever his more light-hearted friends came knocking at his door for him to come out to shoot the breeze or simply goof around, he'd often refuse on the grounds of having chores to complete.

He, however, often partook in organized sports, on which occasions, he played hard and competitively, giving vent to his abundant energy and pent-up anger. He had energy to spare on that evening he happened to walk by a Seville orange tree and noticed that a number of young oranges had fallen to the ground beneath the tree. He kicked one to see how far it would go, then another with added drive to beat the first distance, and so on and on till some twenty odd oranges were kicked far and wide and all the fallen oranges were kicked away. He was decidedly of an athletic bent and build, as well as stamina and aptitude. It was with the alacrity of an acrobatic stunt that he sprung up from his fall after tumbling headlong from his mother's lady's-wheel bicycle while coming down the slope behind the churchyard.

It should not be hard for you to believe that Calvin used considerable diligence making his own slingshot, and that it became his favorite toy, whereas his GI Joe his uncle Owen sent him from America, was only a close runner-up in his affections. With his slingshot, he could aim and fire at objects and obtain satisfaction whenever he hit his target, or if he missed it, he'd be motivated to improve his sighting. Either way, satisfaction would be achieved.

Over the years ever since Calvin was a baby and his father's brother, Owen Brown and his wife, had started reporting on the prosperity they were experiencing as citizens of the United States of America after having emigrated there and lived for some fifteen years, the Browns' interest in following in their footsteps had increased to the point at which they initiated the process of emigration to the U.S. Owen and his wife Thelma were eligible sponsors who were willing and anxious to help the Browns obtain their Green Cards, even though the procedure would be confusing and costly. Good health and moral character, and a favorable disposition toward the U.S., were attributes that would contribute to the successful outcome of the application. After a period of two long years, Calvin and his parents were elated beyond words with the prospects of moving abroad, as any red-blooded Jamaican would have been. America was viewed as the land of golden opportunities, a land where the grass was the greenest in the whole wide world.

As fate would have it, the Browns arrived in New York City on March 4, 1990 to take up residence in America. They would stay with their sponsors until they found a home they could call their own. They would soon settle in their own quarters, not too far from Owen's place, in the community of Bedford-Stuyvesant, an area not predominantly peopled by African Americans, and which is located in the borough of Brooklyn. They found the new experience of being in America, though at times a bit intimidating, charged with the excitement of change and freshness, and the fulfillment of a dream.

Calvin had bounced back from an emotional setback that ensued when he realized that he was one year older than the average age of the grade six class into which he was incorrectly assigned. His teacher was brought to rectify the situation by moving him up into the seventh grade when she discovered that his writing skills were actually superior to those of his classmates who outdid him only in oral expression. The child native to America is more vocal, outspoken and opinionated than Calvin would have been: characteristics that speak volumes for a lack of know-how.

His mother Joyce, was pursuing a course of studies that would qualify her for a career in practical nursing, as she was ambitious of working in a home for the elderly, while his father was gainfully employed as a watchman at a warehouse. They were juggling money to make ends meet at this time, but the forcast for the future painted a rosier picture.

Calvin had never lost his passion for the game of baseball he used to play in some backyard back in Jamaica, utilizing the base of a leaf from the coconut tree as bat, and a green orange as ball. He was happy too, to find Brooklyn a hotbed of baseball, offering him easy opportunity to play the game. He regretted that the home-grown team that emerged as the famous Dodgers had left Brooklyn for Los Angeles, California. On the whole, he missed the year-round opportunity to play outdoors in comfortable weather that Jamaica afforded. On reflection, life seemed lighter in the good old days, when it was easier for him to laugh.

Calvin's tendency toward becoming a serious young man had, however, intensified. He never told jokes, and could hardly endure listening to them, nearly always missing the punch line. For him, the telling of jokes seemed a frivolous exercise when there were always more important things to be done. Yet, he was not an unhappy boy, it just appeared that way on the outside. On the inside, a part of him was accepting being other than serious. In time, Calvin would have to learn to accept that activities he once considered nonsensical, were not only normal, but actually beneficial for one's wellbeing. For leisure, Calvin had become devoted to stamp-collecting, taking pride in the law and order afforded by the hobby, as well as quite enjoying his mental escapes to foreign places, if only in his dreams by way of pictures. He was entertaining desires to travel to faraway places for the sake of exploration of new lifestyles and experiences. A decision to travel and explore America would take him on a trip to California to visit his aunt in San Francisco, but this was not to take place until the year 2003.

In the year 1995, Calvin graduated from high school and made his parents extremely proud of this achievement. Whereas his mother felt he should pursue any postgraduate and praiseworthy course of action that would make him happy, his dad remained dead set on the hope of him going straightway to college or university. Mr. Buck was to remain a patient father for the present time while Calvin would fulfill his desire to take a year off to see the rest of America and to make some educated decisions regarding career options for himself.

Calvin allowed a couple of months after his graduation to pass by without any serious effort on his part to begin his search for salaried employment. He opened his vista to the job market to include casual as well as manual labor. Still living in the family home, he not only contributed to the financial upkeep and running of the home from money he earned doing odd jobs, ranging from valet parking to cleaning cars at a car rental place, but had enough left over to spend on his modest needs. His income, however, was insufficient to encourage a plan to save toward his future education at a college.

A Hodgepodge of Reflections

A desire to increase his earning power and put an end to his cycle of uninspiring jobs, gave birth to his decision to learn a lucrative craft of interest to him. There was much yet for him to learn about the use of the computer, and he reasoned he should get with the times and learn a computer skill. Somewhere in his future this skill would prove useful he reasoned, whether in the home or in the workplace, as the use of the computer was not only on the increase, but universal and inescapable.

The incident of 9/11 came on September 11th, 2001, when the twin towers of the World Trade Center complex were toppled to ground zero by hijacked airliners, sweeping New Yorkers, and in fact all Americans generally speaking, off their feet into a frenzy of disbelief. The towers were a powerful symbol of achievement in international trade and commerce, besides being monuments of pride and grace, especially for New Yorkers.

The Browns were not personally involved in the catastrophy, but remained horror-struck, open-mouthed and glued to their TV set. Calvin was harboring feelings of revenge against the Arab perpetrators who inflicted this horrific act against his adopted city. It was as though New York City had suddenly become his best friend that was wronged. A new-born consciousness of his affection for the city was being realized.

Sometime after the fall of the twin towers, and America's engagement with shock had advanced into rage, President George W. Bush, supported by his advisors, the Vice President Dick Cheney and the Secretary of Defense, Donald Rumsfeld, began to make public their plan to launch a non-retaliatory military air strike and invasion of the Republic of Iraq. The rage of the American people brought on by the destruction of the twin towers, provided the opportune time for the Bush Administration to sow the seeds of revenge amongst the people against Saddam, who they were blaming for sheltering the likes of the perpetrators. It was his pumped-up puppet of a spokesman, Secretary of State, Colin Powell, who was used to report to the American people, and indeed the rest of the world, with full verbal and pictorial illustrations, giving reasons in support of the decision to invade this potentially dangerous country that threatened the safety of Americans.

The aim of the Bush Administration was to topple the autocratic leadership of Saddam Hussein, who they charged with providing sanctuary for terrorists and conspiring with them against the West. The main accusations were that he was secretly building an atomic bomb and producing agents of biological warfare.

The fact that Saddam had in the past committed acts of atrocity against his own people, was pointed out repeatedly in the effort to further smear his character and turn public opinion against him and also used as a means of adding fuel to the case they were building against him. Saddam Hussein was built up to be America's number-one enemy, and it was hoped that somewhere in his neighborhood lurked Osama bin Laden and his cohorts.

To find a headquarters of an organization of terrorists that could be dismantled and destroyed, was a target of desire. However, the will -o'- the - wisp character of terrorism, makes it impossible for one to organize its demise. It has been found that the prime recruit within a western country for engagement in terrorist activities against his state, comes not only from the Muslim citizens who have not found a secure footing in their society, but also from alienated and angered citizens of the host country. Because these potential terrorists spring up from within the borders of their respective countries, it stands to reason, that no program designed to secure these borders against the infiltration of terrorists, can be foolproof.

Local participants in terrorism are not necessarily motivated into action by a desire to defend the faith of Islam, but by a desire to give vent to feelings of inadequacy engendered by their life circumstances. They are attracted to the violent, apocalyptic fervor of the extremists which provide a fitting vehicle of expression for venting their anger. It is true that the presence of western peacekeeping troops serving in Muslim countries, and the invasion of Iraq, may be viewed by the potential terrorist as a "Zionist-Crusader assault on Islam" to certain susceptible young Muslims. Incidents of local terrorist attacks are invariably suspected to have been masterminded by an international network, namely al-Qaeda. But they are, in fact, scattered incidents following an ideological and tactical template that was created by Osama bin Laden: so, in a very limited sense, every attack has an al-Qaeda link. However, the central organization itself is no longer an active player. Sporadic terrorist attacks carried out in western countries will continue as long as western troops are stationed in Muslim countries and the Israeli-Palestinian issue remains unresolved.

The world was divided into two, as it were, those in favor of the looming attack, and those who opposed it. The latter group included hundreds of thousands from around the world who publicly demonstrated against it. Amongst the main dissenting countries, were Germany, France and Canada. These countries, as well as others, were not in support of military action on the grounds of its illegality: since the decision to invade was not sanctioned under the charter of the United Nations Organization, and furthermore, because of the heightening uncertainty concerning the validity of the source of the information that led to charges laid against the Iraquis.

The Browns who had declared themselves Democrats, listened to the conflicting, never-ending rhetoric around them, and finding themselves in a state of confusion, refrained from taking sides in favor or against the proposed war. Their state of uncertainty was to be intensified with the loud speculation that accused Mr. Bush and his administration for acting on the motive to seize control over Iraq's copious oil reserves, thereby to establish a broader presence and ultimate control over the Middle East. And would this act not constitute what is called imperialism?

Would it not be advantageous for America to secure a military base in Iraq within the geographic proximity to the Gulf Cooperation Council countries of Saudi Arabia, Bahrain, Kuwait, Oman, Qatar, and the United Arab Emirates: countries in which America has bases with stockpiles of armament and strategic control? Bringing Iraq into the fold of allies, would put an end to feelings of uncertainty held by America regarding the place it holds in that country's esteem.

The degree of doubt, indicated by the magnitude of the opposition to the war on different fronts, triggered a new need to invent additional reasons to substantiate the original claims of need to undertake military action. The Bush administration implemented a new strategy, and a new rationale that offered the people of Iraq a 'regime change' that would bring with it a new freedom and a democratic society. Because Americans treasure certain freedoms of action as a right embodied in the principles of democracy, it was prudent for the Administration to incorporate the idea of freeing the Iraquis from the tyrannical rule under Saddam Hussein. There was a need to drum up more support on the home front for the plan to go to war. No wonder that the war was officially named 'Operation Iraqi Freedom'.

It hardly seems feasible that a superpower would undertake the monumental mission of a military invasion of a country across continents, and pay dearly in treasure and human lives, simply because it wants to introduce democracy to a people or to remove its dictator. This objective to democratize, could be perceived as a cover to a hidden agenda. Could this desire to spread democracy to a country have sprung from a deep-seated paranoia that what was different in the Arab was of potential danger to the national safety of Americans? If this were so, any attempt to spread a way of life and a set of values amongst a people under the name of democracy, would be understandable. But would it not prove more effective, and definitely less costly and less painful, to allow the natural process of osmosis, (or infiltration), and exemplary behavior along with gestures of goodwill and friendliness, to be the means of accomplishing this end? Democracy cannot be delivered from the muzzle of a gun!

Unlike his parents, Calvin, now a fledgling idealist who was longing for a world of justice and moral order, chose wholeheartedly to support the idea of war. A radicalized young American was motivated to embark on the secret pleasure of wiping out evil at the root.

It is conceivable that Calvin's simplistic view for solving the problem of terrorism, is identical to that held by Mr. Bush, and which view engenders the motivations of their stance. They both envision Americans as the good guys who should not allow what they categorize as evil to flourish in Iraq. They are persuaded by their conscience to pay the price of opposing what they see as evil. They see only the color black, or alternatively, the color white, and never the possibility of a blending of the two colors into shifting shades of gray, where alternatives could abound. They pat themselves on the shoulder and say, it's all about being a decent human being. Mr. Bush is a man who prides himself on his changelessness and regards immutability as his outstanding virtue. He being such a man, would resist implementing a change in policy, even when faced with chaos as a result of his erroneous actions. He would resist using psychology to develop an adroit policy to win shifting alliances over to America's side instead to trying to alienate them. He would have no clue that his own headlong and heedless actions in the Middle East would contribute to the deepening chaos there, and his own diminished leverage on the world stage.

Calvin had gathered enough steam and cash to push on with his plan to visit his aunt in San Francisco. He was delighted at the prospect of having the use of her old, beaten-up Ford to get around the area, so long as he bought his own gasoline and was responsible for repairs, should the Mustang break down. He was also looking forward to moving away from the discouraging atmosphere of his home where his parents were dampening his aspirations of joining the Marines. Besides his natural inclinations, the benefits of serving as a soldier as observed from TV, were most attractive to him. He was especially interested in the G I Bill Program by which he could receive money toward a college education.

After 9/11 no one was hiring workers in New York City, and also Calvin had grown despondent with his vicious cycle of odd jobs, living partly dependent on his parents from paycheck to paycheck. Not only had he reached the breaking point with his woeful-go-around of temporary jobs, but to be totally frank, he had yielded to the temptation to join the military as a quick-fix-solution to his problem, and the easiest way he saw out of the rut in which he had started to stagnate. He figured after all, that the short two-year period would provide the break from the cycle of monotony of his life, and more importantly, bring him a sense of accomplishment and worthy recognition. He was indeed, inspired to act on the message implied in the recruiting commercial: 'Be all that you can be. It is not just a job, but an adventure.'

In San Francisco, Calvin liked what he observed to be a less metropolitan city than New York. San Francisco offered more openness, roadways that climbed or descended gently over hills, and beaches with palm trees that provided a scenery reminiscent of those he left behind in Jamaica. On the whole, the vibe of the city with its old Victorian houses, hole-in-the-wall shops, —- and even the homeless on the streets, —- captivated him.

Calvin was surprised at the number of uniformed recruiting officers he saw at street corners in the vicinity of high school, college or university, talking and smiling while handing out pamphlets to young men passing by, as though they were promoting a Club Med vacation. Monetary as well as prestigious rewards for membership in the armed forces were being promoted and elaborated on, in the streets of San Francisco.

In 2003, he was out and about doing touristic things such as exploring the Golden Gate Park and seeing the seals at the Fisherman's Wharf when he and his

A Hodgepodge of Reflections

cousin of the same age as himself, ran into a marine recruiting station located at Pleasant Hill. The men decided to go into the station just to check it out and get the feel of the place with the intention of returning the following day for more serious inquiries. The day was already too far spent, and they were too tired to bother attempting further investigation.

The following day, he was told by the Marine Corps outfit that he would have had to wait one month for an interview due to an influx of applications. Across from the Marine recruiting station, he spotted a recruiting station for the Army, with fervent recruiters standing about the entrance door with open arms to attract his attention. Calvin in his eagerness, decided on the spot to join the Army instead. His feelings of resolve to fight the good fight were bolstered by the rather prominent poster on the wall of the recruiting office which said: 'Every generation has its heroes, this one is no different.'

Calvin was not totally surprised to find that his interview with the Army recruiting officer was like no other he had had before for a job. He was made to feel, not only effusively welcomed, but that his decision to serve was greatly laudible and highly appreciated. His preliminary interview leading up to the moment of signing on the dotted line went by without a hitch, as his responses to questions regarding criminal record, standard of education, the possession of tattoos, drug habit, et cetera, presented no obstacles that might delay the progress of his enlistment. He later learned, however, that most hurdles that stood in the way of enlistment, such as the possession of a minor criminal record, could be removed by the wave of a magic wand or the signing of waivers. No stone would have been left unturned in an effort to ease an applicant through the process. They were that hard up for applicants.

So far, Calvin was pleased with the prospects of becoming a soldier, and found the idea of serving only the two years required by the Army instead of the four years required by the Marine Corps, plus the four-thousand-dollar signing bonus he would receive, most agreeable. For the next two years, he was to be housed, clothed and fed with full medical and dental benefits, in addition to a monthly salary. If he were married, he would have been eligible for a Basic Allowance for Housing of over thirteen hundred dollars per month.

Calvin was able to go without delay to the military Entrance Processing Station to complete the initial paperwork and medical tests required for enlistment. His score in the Armed Services Vocational Aptitude Battery test made him eligible for a two-year service, and his sufficiently high General Technical score gave him the option of choosing any job in the Army at the entry level.

Two months after enlisting and taking of the oath to defend the Constitution of the United States against enemies both foreign and domestic, he was called for training as a member of the Bravo Company, 1st Battalion of the 50th Infantry Regiment which would locate at Fort Benning, Georgia.

One of Calvin's first duties after entering basic training, was to forward a form letter to his parents, worded by the Commander of the Battalion, informing them of his undertaking which promised to be rigorous and of the highest standard, and assuring them of the military's constant vigil over his safety and wellbeing, and imploring them to support his noble efforts by way of keeping in touch with him by correspondence.

Mr. and Mrs. Brown, at that point, had grown mostly accepting of Calvin's decision, with the normal parental concerns. Mrs. Brown, the more yielding and less outwardly emotional of the two, had quietly cut the apron strings that bound her to her son, while Mr. Brown, had gradually conditioned his opposing heart, coming to terms with his true feelings with the conclusion that his son's actions resulted from his having grown up in America.

During the fourteen weeks of training at Fort Benning, Calvin took to the physical exhaustion and the test of endurance imposed upon him by his trainers, like a duck to water. He had a hard time, however, growing accustomed to the habitual cursing and yelling on the part of the drill sergeants. Needless to say that much skill, discipline and information were passed on from trainer to trainee.

Hoping that life at the military post at Fort Lewis in the state of Washington would bring a welcome change to the arduousness of basic training at Fort Benning, Calvin was anxious to move on to the next leg on his way to Iraq. No time had been lost in informing the recruits that they were to be deployed to the Middle East after the in-processing session, which would last about one week, and further training and briefing at Fort Lewis. After his in-processing, he was assigned to the Tomahawk Battalion comprising the Army's first-ever Stryker Combat Team.

After the 0630 run on October the 16th, the men were herded into the Carey Theatre to heed the passionate pep talk delivered by the battalion Commander, designed to infuse zeal into the fighting spirit of the men. The Commander had the reputation of a Spartan warrior with deep moral convictions, and who was prodigiously well read in history, philosophy and maps. His resume listed only his commands and no other career paraphernalia. The fear-imparting speech left Calvin modifying his concept of a peacekeeping roll in Iraq to that of offensive operations and the countering of ambushes. Calvin was able to buffer his growing concerns about what to expect from his assignment to Iraq, with his innate resilience that assured him that he would rise to any occasion whenever it arose.

Later, they were briefed on how to deal with the media and what the responses to certain specific questions should be. Answers to the likely questions were based on the purpose of their mission to Iraq. They were seriously briefed regarding the purpose of their mission to Iraq, which was to liberate from bondage, and bring freedom to the Iraqis, to restore independence, to eliminate the enemy, and to continue the Global War on Terrorism. They would remain in Iraq until the mission was complete. To achieve these ends, the liberator had to be friendly and respectful to the civilian, and to show mindfulness of his property. On the other hand, however, the soldier was to be prepared to defend his own life and to protect his property as

A Hodgepodge of Reflections

well. They were given an acronym for the dual task of winning hearts and minds and nation-building. The buzzword was SASO, stemming from the term 'Stability and Security Operations.' Answers to the questions that the media might ask were issued to them on a piece of green card-stock paper that they were to fold up and place in their wallets. Other Public Affairs guidance was given, concerning military vehicles sush as the Stryker and other equipment.

Before deployment to a combat zone, it was mandatory for Calvin's unit to attend a two-and-a-half-week field training session, which was to be held at the Joint Readiness Training Centre at Fort Polk in Louisiana. Training would basically be one huge war game, where death and resurrection were played out with simulated firefights using blanks. In preparation for departure to Joint Readiness Training, packing lists of items they would require for the exercise were issued. The items were to be laid out for inspection by the squad or team leader before they were to be fitted into duffel bags and rucksacks.

Calvin had his turn at playing dead and getting carried away to the casualty-collecting point, but nothing compared to his sitting behind the M240 Bravo: the fully automatic machine gun, which he hoped to operate in the Iraq war. Despite the fact that the skills learned by serving in the infantry as a gunner were not useful in procuring employment in the outside world, Calvin had his heart set on being a gunner, or at least serving on the weapons squad.

Because Calvin took pride in whatever task he was assigned, and was ambitious of being the fittest of them all, he would go to the gym, which was free for soldiers, and do extra physical training. Drawing from his strong scholastic past, he was able to devote considerable time to studying his training and field manuals from cover to cover. This latter endeavor gave him an edge over his peers, and made a favorable impression on his superiors. It was easy for Calvin to stand out intellectually above most of his peers because of his high intelligence. Calvin would prove Hunter S. Thompson's statement, that says that soldiery is 'almost wholly composed of dullards and intellectual sluggards,' and that it 'is a painful hell for anyone with an IQ over 80', inapplicable to his state of circumstance.

Calvin with his show of gift and natural inclinations, was assigned to Platoon Pentagon, made up of the usual four squads, one of which was the weapons squad under the leadership of Sergeant Peter Green. Peter, the guy everyone grew to like, was never silent. He was a 'radio' of his past military accomplishments and of his gun-management expertise, in the nicest possible manner, that did not offend the listener or grate on his nerves. Calvin hung to Peter's every word of recountal and learned nearly all there was to learn about the use of the M240 Bravo machine gun, two of which were designated to each platoon. Calvin's keenness on guns made him an obvious choice to be one of the two gunners of the Platoon Pentagon. Each of the two gun teams of the squad employed a gunner, an assistant gunner and an ammo bearer, to serve under a gun-team leader.

At this juncture, Calvin had yet another lesson to learn. In order to prevent the loss of the many expensive items of equipment a soldier carries around on his person during combat, he must learn the technique of tying down these items with 5/50 survival cord using specialized knots, that would, for example, attach his watch to his sleeve, and his earplug container to his flak jacket, and so on, until every item he was carrying would be tied to something.

Just killing spare time window-shopping, he was staring at he gadgets exhibited in the showcase at the AAFES PX, when he raised his gaze to glance at the face beside his. It was the round and chubby face that appeared permanently on the verge of breaking into a smile, and that he had seen before at basic training. The face belonged to a strapping body commanding a second glance and posing a contrast to the bearer's jovial disposition. With the need for companionship, Calvin followed his urge and took the initiative to introduce himself to Derek Abuwi, who himself, seemed at a loss for companionship. Both men were to spend the rest of the evening getting to know each other. Derek's parents came to America from war-torn Lebanon and passed on more than a working knowledge of the Arabic language to their son. Derek, like himself, had grown tired of knocking around from pillar to post, and wanted to do something he figured important and honorable with his life. He too saw joining the Army as an answer to his need. He, like Calvin, was willing to sacrifice two years of his life in order to earn college money. Another sacrifice Derek had to make was to give up the habits of cigarette smoking and boozing, which were forbidden by Army regulations. Dishwashing and tree cutting, however, he gladly left behind him.

Calvin's laugh at one of Derek's jokes lost its punch as the image of his recently acquired tattoo popped into his mind. The meta tag tattooed in his arm pit bearing his name, Social Security number, blood type and religion, would serve to identify him in the event of his being shattered beyond recognition, by land mine or an improvised explosive device at the hands of the enemy. The knowledge that his parents, whom he had named as his beneficiaries, would receive one-quarter of a million dollars from the U.S. government in the case of his death, was of very little comfort to him.

Calvin would not let anyone know of the nightmares he was experiencing as a result of having watched explicit videos on terrorist training. He also found his surrounding atmosphere charged with an undercurrent of fear, often vocally expressed by his comrades as hostility toward those Iraqis who might oppose the freedom movement. Moments of uncertainty about his decision to go to war, were fleeting and infrequent, but mostly he was comfortable with it, especially when he was having a good time with his peers.

The perfectionist in Calvin was left feeling inadequately prepared to communicate with the Iraqi, having had only a one-hour lesson in the Arabic language on the day they were handed their deployment orders to Iraq, which was to be on the 13th of November 2003. Today too, Calvin got busy on the telephone to break the news to his parents and friends regarding his deployment to a place called the Suuni

A Hodgepodge of Reflections

Triangle in Iraq. At this crucial moment, his parents managed to be outwardly calm, wishing him all the best, without letting on of their deep-seated fears for his safety.

Recollections of life at the base in Fort Lewis grew vague and distant to Private Calvin Brown sitting on a civilian plane taking off from the McChord Air Force Base bound for the Rhein Air Force Base in Germany. Surprisingly, his most recurring recall of life at the base, was not his sitting behind the M240 Bravo gun, but the rain that fell daily there, in the middle of a rain forest as it were.

On arrival at the Rhine AFB at 3:30 AM local time, Calvin was surprised to find the base buzzing with life, and packed with soldiers in desert camouflage, all headed for Kuwait like himself, or Afghanistan. That night, a can of coke in hand, Calvin was feeling important as they boarded a flight to Kuwait, dressed in full uniform, duffel bags and weapons placed under their seats with the gun barrels pointed away from the aisle and the bolts removed. Being too excited for sleep, Calvin watched a movie on TV called 'The Hunt for Red October' starring Sean Connery. They descended over Kuwait at noon the next day, just in time to look out at the endless monotony of ashen desert in every direction under a clear and sunny sky.

On the ground in Kuwait City, the soldiers were loaded into buses driven by natives, and were told to keep the window shades closed all the way to Camp Wolf. The first order of business on arrival at the camp, was to swipe their ID cards through a machine that would automatically activate a method of payment of their combat wages.

There was no tarrying for the exhausted men at Camp Wolf, as they were soon to embark on a three-and-one-half hours ride to Camp Udari in the northwest of the Kuwait desert. This camp is the American staging point for the marine deployments to Iraq. All the chatter on the bus heading north for Camp Udari, simmered down into silence as the jet fatigued soldiers all fell into deep sleep. Whenever Calvin awoke, he would look around to see his peers asleep or staring about with bleary-eyes.

They arrived at Camp Udari at midnight. Next morning after the early battalion run in the desert sand, the men had a formation in front of a conex, a large shipping container, upon which the battalion Commander climbed, and gave one of his motivational speeches, as he had done before at Fort Lewis. He made no effort to soften the bombshell he delivered in his command that scheduled the men to do raids in the worse possible areas in Iraq, where insurgency was on the increase with the entry of insurgents from Iran and Syria.

The madness of war was in the air, and it was contagious. Calvin found his immunity to feelings of aggression weakening under the pressure of the immediacy of confronting the growing threats of insurgent hostility in Iraq. Frenzied, idle talk expressing thoughts of blowing up camels that crossed the desert, or pointing the muzzle of their guns up into Miss America when she came for the Thanksgiving Day celebrations to sing and serve turkey dinner to the guys, was heard coming from the soldiers. Some of the same men were seen wiping tears from their eyes as Miss America sang God Bless America crying. The veneer had fallen from their faces to reveal their youth and vulnerability. Let it be imagined that these young and impressionable minds would be capable of killing innocent civilians, for after all, the many men represented the many backgrounds of society, and this being the case, such a possibility was a reality.

Calvin was finding the mixed messages regarding peacekeeping versus offensive action upsetting. But small wisdom brought him to the calming decision to live one day at a time, and that day, well-lived, without undue projection into the future. For the next month, he must face life at Camp Udari engaged in the arduous task of filling sandbags to line the floors of the Humvees and the trucks, so that if ever they got hit by an IED, the sandbags would absorb some of the concussion and shrapnel. This strenuous reality was only to be worsened by the disagreeableness of the living conditions they encountered at the camp.

Camping in the tent city of Camp Udari in the midst of the Kuwaiti desert, might under normal circumstances hold a sense of adventure, but in the advent of war, this was not the general mood amongst the troops. The nauseating overflowing Porta-Johns, plus the intermittent supply of electric lighting and water, were downers that frustrated the men. The unavailability of alcoholic beverages and cigarettes for purchase, coupled with the fact that they were not allowed to smoke inside the flammable tents, were also conditions the men found inconvenient. They slept on cots set out under the world of tents supplied by the Kellog, Brown and Root company positioned behind the two quarter-mile-long lines of seven-ton trucks and Humvees stretching across the horizon and pointing north toward Baghdad.

Before setting the convoy in motion, however, yet another attempt to use scriptural inferences with the intent of sanctifying the war undertaking, and of bolstering the fortitude of the soldier, was staged by a surrogate Chaplain. He read from the so-called warrior psalm, Psalm 91: 'He is my refuge and my fortress .... A thousand shall fall at thy side, and ten thousand at thy right hand; but it shall not come nigh thee.' The Chaplain continued: 'Remember, you're on the enemy's playground, the terrain of evil. To trust in the Lord is the best way to hunt down the devil.' Some men yawned in reaction to this reading, saying under the breath 'sure' , with true connotation of that word, while Calvin, a man who like his father, revered the Bible, became contemplative. The morale of the men living and serving in austere conditions, counting the days when they would return home, could not be boosted on polite subtleties or secular philosophy, but only on the stark belief in their own righteousness and the iniquity of their enemy.

Set for Baghdad, the largest troop movement with roughly 250,000 soldiers and marines, entering Iraq through the desert from Kuwait, would constitute one of history's last great military convoys. An achievement that called to mind the 10,000 Greek hoplites under Xenophon, who marched from Mesopotamia across Asia Minor in 400 B.C., hacking their way through every army that challenged them.

A Hodgepodge of Reflections

The convoy traveled north for two hours along the main route, Highway 80, and rolled into Navistar, located along the Kuwaiti border. Navistar is the massive refueling and maintenance facility located on a gravel maze of Jersey barriers that smelled of oil and gasoline, and the last refueling stop made on that side of the chain-link fences separating Kuwait from Iraq.

The immensity of the redeployment at this juncture was visually staggering, and made even more amazing by the buzzing of engines and generators. Here the troops did a march in formation to the chow hall, which was airless and overcrowded with low ceilings and putrefying smells. At night the men slept on sleeping bags laid on the sand between the lines of vehicles, and were awakened at 2:30 A.M. to leave without washing themselves or using the toilet, due to the absence of running water and Porta-Johns. They packed their gears in the dark, fiddling with straps and lubricants, cursing at broken doors and transmission problems. As was customary on such occasions, the troops were briefed. One of the directives they received was a request for them to take Gatorade bottles along to urinate in, as they would only be making scheduled stops along the way for this purpose, when they could all water the desert in unison.

The convoy was not just a line of vehicles, but a functional assemblage of coordinated components of ground combat, aviation, command, support services and journalists, all bound together by a common purpose of mission, and thus cemented by comradeship. The scholar, the cook and the tattooed were brought to share much more than common quarters. Another connecting link between the units were the briefings and commands delivered over the handheld ICOMs or the intra-squad radios.

Calvin was a bundle of emotions: personal fear of danger, that warm cozy feeling of belonging, and resignation to a worthy undertaking, all tightly wrapped in one packet. Sitting in the back of a Humvee behind a M240 Bravo machine gun as a machine gunner, Calvin's job was to keep both eyes wide open for lurking threats, especially at freeway overpasses from which vantage point enemies habitually hurled life-threatening weapons onto passing troops. This job placed the men in mortal danger to guard the convoy along a nerve-racking obstacle course of booby traps, car bombs, and other deadly weapons.

Calvin was somewhat comforted by the hovering of Army Kiowa helicopters flying over the convoy, up and down the freeway like bees, providing another watchdog for danger signals. Up to this point, all Calvin had noticed on the overpass was a large graffiti in English that said: 'Fuck you Americans! ———-Mohammed.' He had also noticed that the road signs were in Arabic with the English translation below. Calvin had hoped to see camels, but settled for men in robes and Keiffiyahs standing beside sheep and cattle, waving with welcoming gestures. He found this sign of approval of the invasion heartening, though with a grain of caution.

Entering Iraq was like visiting another planet. In the dark of night, Iraq was heralded by lights of burning petrol fires, while the light of day presented a terrain of bare spaces as far as the eye could see for miles and miles, and much later, of dried mud oases with white-out date palm jungles, and of houses that appeared to be made from a mixture of mud and garbage. In the early evening, the sun sank so fast over the desert it was like a searchlight being switched off. At nights the freezing north-east wind cooled the semi-tropical desert air to an unbearable cold. This dreary landscape did not let up with the appearance of the meandering muddy waters of the Tigris and Euphrates rivers, that feed the many lakes and turgid mud - swamps, all caught in a mire across the flats.

Thirteen hours after leaving Navistar , the convoy pulled into the U.S. military fueling and resupply depot of Scania, two hours south of Baghdad near Al-Hillah. Again the men slept on the gravel between the vehicles in sleeping bags against the shivering cold. Calvin slept in a sort of half-sleep and awoke early to roll with the convoy entering Baghdad through a snarling traffic jam in the densely populated area, that brought added concerns because of the many begging kids that swarmed the humvees for handouts. The men had been instructed to turn a deaf ear to this source of nuisance.

Calvin thought that it was a shame that the many Sunni and Shiite mosques, with their glittering faience domes, that once stood for the golden age of Baghdad at the turn of the century, were being desecrated by their use as millitant operational hideouts by ememy forces.

No sooner had Calvin arrived to the Sunni Triangle area, was his Platoon assigned to take up temporary residence at the FOB (forward operating base) of Pacesetter, from which base he would be forwarded to carry out the duty of the military operation of securing the area surrounding a mosque suspected of housing noncompliants to the American invasion. Orders to launch the mission were passed down to the platoon and squad leaders in the war room, were the details of the OP were discussed in details with the aid of maps, et cetera. Once the plan of the mission was completed, it was passed on to the squad members.

It would be one of the duties of the infantry to watch out for resistants bearing arms, to pull additional security onto their position, and in the case where detainees were held, to escort them to the command post for questioning.

As the vehicle they were traveling in sped toward the area of operation, Calvin was excited by an adrenaline rush when all he could hear over and over again on the radio in a woman's voice was: 'Warning! Enemy in area!' In the meanwhile, the men in the Stryker were viewing a graphic map of the area on a computer screen, that would show the location of the enemy, as indicated by the apperance of a red triangle that would pop into view whenever contact with the enemy was electronically reported.

As they raced as fast as they could to where the crossfires were taking place, several burned remains of cars were seen on the road. The area seemed deserted with the storefronts and apartment buildings on the main street closed.

On arrival to the area, they moved their vehicle over to the front of the mosque

A Hodgepodge of Reflections

where a closer view of the damage done by the thousands and thousands of rounds of explosives, instilled a fear for the worse yet to come. To the left of their vehicle was one Platoon, and to the left of them another Platoon, and to their left, was the MGS (missile guidance set) and mortars, all engaging the mosque. Calvin and West pulled rear security, facing away from the site of the action, in order to scan their sector and make sure nobody tried to shoot at their men from behind. The shooting at the mosque came in waves with alternating barrages followed by periods of silence, then a thunderous explosion of a TOW missile impacted the mosque, lighting up the sky, but did not take the tower down, like it would have in the movies.

After the missile explosion and sustained bombardment of the mosque, the attacks slowed down, and orders went out for the men to move in and to secure the perimeter of the building. The dismounted Bravo Victor 21 spotted an insurgent in the tower, at which time, the men reopened fire on the tower until several rounds of ammunition expended.

On such exercises, it was customary for an Iraqi translator, an imbedded reporter to report on the mission from a first hand point of view, as well as a combat medic, to go along on the mission. It was the duty of the combat medic on this occasion, to pronounce the body of a young guy, his mouth and eyes wide open, and having a stereotypical Al Qaeda terrorist beard, as dead. The medic also reported that the walls and flooring of the mosque were literally covered with chunks and pieces of human body parts, and that was the reason why only one of the insurgents was recognizable as a person. On the war zone of total destructuon were thousands of brass castings, missile wires, chunks of concrete, cars completely blown to bits or overturned, huge craters in the ground sculpted by car-bomb explosions.

The thought that this undertaking might demonstrate the principle of overkill did occur to Calvin. He was appalled too at the idea of having fired at a holy place of worship causing excessive collateral damage to its structure. Though this act in principle was contrary to American military policy in Iraq, this whole exercise could be used as an example of how wrong a war can go when the soldier is faced with the situation of self-defence or having to prove his worth. At this moment Calvin would rather have been attending his church back home.

That evening, the men returned to Pacesetter to endure the harshest living conditions they had encountered up to that point. There were no showers, running water, recreational facilities, shops, or Porta-Johns. Only circus tents, sleeping cots, communal makeshift outhouses with removable poop barrels, and PVC pipes driven into the ground for urinals. The men were counting on the expectation that they would soon be posted to a new base in the immediate future, since it was the practice of the military to move units with startling frequency from base to base as required to carry out the various missions. Let it be known, however, that the food served to the troops, would pass the strictest test for quality and taste. Eggs, bacon and sausages for breakfast, and with a stretch of the imagination, steak and lobster for Sunday dinner.

Reveille was at 5:30 A.M., followed by a briefing regarding the next combat assignment. On an alert to the city of Samarra, the men would be kicking down doors street by street, block by block, while Calvin under the direction of Special Grant, would be tasked out to the guys in mortars on the outskirts of the city. His job as an infantryman, would be to pull security on the troops in the city.

In response, they loaded into the Strykers and left through the gate, when they were halted and given the news about the Stryker of the 3rd Platoon ahead of them, that had driven off the road and landed upside down in a ditch full of water. The occupants were unable to pry the doors open and consequently, three marines perished. Calvin was not only sad to hear this news, but discouraged that three of the men he knew by name were actually dead.

The very next day, Calvin and his peers heard some news he thought would be beneficial to him. He was hoping that if Saddam Hussein was captured, it might mean that the war could soon come to an end. However, the First Sergent Neil, assured him that the capture of the Iraqi leader would make no difference to their engagement, since they were there not just to topple the head of government, but to establish an imperialistic footing into the unpredictable future. Saddam was imprisonment, tried and sentenced to death for crimes against humanity committed against his people. With the sanction of the Americans, he was put to death by hanging on December 30, 2006, at the hands of the Iraqi Interim Government. His dream to have talks over tea with the leader of the free world, for the mere honor of the occasion: if not in an effort to alleviate his fears, was interred with his bones.

The more stringent ROEs (rules of engagement) imposed on the city, were loosened concerning the curfew placed on the citizens, and instead of shooting those caught on the street between midnight and 6 A.M., they were to be detained instead. The first day was uneventful. Just after midnight, however, two men were brought to the command post for questioning. One was found to be drunk, and the other to be mentally retarded.

On another occasion, soldiers tried to stop a suspicious dilapidated 'Beamer' by loudly yelling and gesturing to the driver, who seemingly unaware of their intent, continued on his way disregarding their request. The soldiers opened fire on the car, which alerted the driver to stop and come out of his vehicle with both hands up and saying 'No, mista! No, mista! Don't shoot!' simultaneously giving the universal sign language for 'I surrender and I'm unarmed.' His eyes were pure unforgettable fear. Shouts of warning coming from a member of the platoon that the surrenderer had something in his hand, triggered the reaction among the soldiers to reopen fire upon him. The Iraqi barber, as he was later found out to be, fell to the ground giving the impression that he had succumbed to bullet wounds. He was approached and handcuffed, and then examined by the combat medic, Doc Dawson, who pronounced him dead. The life had been pelted from the suspected resistant who was found not to be carrying a weapon, but a sign on his car that said: 'God bless America.'

Calvin judged the killing to be a frivolous act indicative of a low regard for

A Hodgepodge of Reflections

human life, and if not, an act governed by a complex of motives, not excluding prejudice and brainwashing. Brainwashing could have started during basic training at Fort Lewis, when the soldiers were made to memorize The Infantryman's Creed: a set of rules of conduct they recited daily, and that had the power to indoctrinate and change the civilian into a cold-blooded infantry killer.

Calvin's take on the killing was upheld by an explanation given by his friend Derek Abuwi, who not only spoke some Arabic, but understood something of the customs of the people, that his fellow troops displayed cultural ignorance in the use of the hand signal used to stop Iraqi drivers, which actually meant 'hello' instead of 'stop' to the Iraqi.

They remained in Samarra for two full weeks, going on combat missions during the day, and sleeping at night on the ground outside their vehicles, with only ponchos and poncho liners to keep them warm. If it rained at night, which was often the case, they would set up the ponchos as tents to keep them dry. Or alternatively, they would sleep in one of the many business buildings appropriated by the U.S. military for use as temporary command posts, that were made vacant by abandonment by their rightful owners or occupants because of the war.

With Calvin's move to FOB St. Mere, he was pleased with the improvements in the living conditions he experienced there over other bases in his past. The chow hall had separate salad and desert bars, a big-screen television, set permanently to the ESPN sports channel, a well-stocked PX for shopping, laundry facilities, shower units and even a soldier's chapel where the launching of military events received the chaplain's benediction, followed by the singing of a hymn to the accompaniment of the bagpipes.

His days at St. Mere were busy. At nights, nevertheless, Calvin found it hard to fall asleep because of the stray dogs barking in the distance, one at a time, or all together like an eerie choir of wailers. And if this barking was not enough to keep him awake, there was the blasting of mournful Arabic music and monotone Koronic readings coming from the tinny speakers in the mosques around the city. These disturbing experiences brought him to the realization that he was indeed a stranger in a strange country far away from home.

FOB Mercury, on the hand, was a bleak gravel and dirt expanse with low reinforced concrete buildings and rows of tents. It was noisy with the groan of generators, frustrating with the busted doors, smashed fluorescent lights and choking dust, and intermittent supply of electricity and running water. A common occurrence was the scavenging for toilet paper and for plastic bottles of drinking water. The poorly lit chow hall with an atmosphere as grim as a penitentiary, allowed only for crowded seating along long tables, and space for their rifles and helmets at their feet.

The first day they were at FOB Mercury, they were attacked by mortars and rockets. As a matter of fact, the distance to the chow hall was the single most dangerous place at the whole base. For this reason, Calvin would occasionally miss meals, not wanting to brave the walk to the chow hall. On these occasions, he would feed his ravenous appetite with potato chips he bought earlier at the PX.

Mortar and rocket attacks from the direction of Al-Fallujah and Al-Karmah necessitated night-long patrols which entailed lingering in a suspect spot, enduring the cold, getting a headache from the night vision goggles, seeing and hearing nothing, returning at dawn fatigued, only to discover that shortly after they had abandoned their post, a mortar was launched from a spot close to the FOB. Don't ask how it was possible for one to get used to the frequent and daily mortar and rocket attacks on the base! Just the same, the guys took them in stride without retaliation. Despite having the technology to pinpoint the origin of an attack and to accurately return fire, no attempt was made to do this, since this action would involve the risk of hurting civilians. The inevitability and frequency of the occurrence conditioned the men who learned to differentiate between the swish and the whistle sounds made by the rockets as they traveled through the air, that told of their proximity as well as their direction.

An attempt to make a list of the names of those soldiers who wished to vote in the upcoming U.S. elections of 2004, failed to come up with a satisfactory number of interested participants. To avoid the occurrence of a high absentee voter turnout, the Army improvised a method to address the problem by demanding the troops to attend a mass formation at early o'clock, bringing with them their ID cards and pens. At the formation, a pep talk on the importance of patriotism was given in an effort to motivate the men to cast their ballots. Tables were set up, registration forms put out, and the soldiers were divided by states and given the option to register themselves. Calvin took up his position at the New York table and volunteered to register to vote, which he would have done, anyway, without the pep talk. Nonetheless, what he found confusing was the question on the paperwork that asked for party affiliation. That was when he decided to write down Independent, even though he had always thought of himself as a Democrat like his parents. Does this gesture on Calvin's part come from feelings of mistrust in the powers that ruled? At this time, a subdued mutter from amongst the inconsequential utterances was heard: 'Vote? Our job is to protect democracy, not be a part of it!'

Calvin had always spent as little time as possible in the latrines at the base, but since the stir over the upcoming U.S. elections, he found himself not only doing what he went in for, but staying behind to read the election-themed graffiti on the walls there: 'Bush lies and soldiers die.' 'The only lies that are true are the ones you believe.' 'Vote for Kerry. Vote to go home.' 'Vote for whomever you want, we are here to stay, dumb ass.'

The Army Commendation Medal (ARCOM) is a mid-level U.S. military award, normally presented for sustained acts of heroism or meritorious service. However, the Army typically authorises the award of the medal for Junior officers and enlisted personnel as an end-of-tour award. At the end of the first year of service, Calvin and his peers were awarded Army Commendation Medals on October 1st, 2004, just about the time the men were to return to their homes in America for

A Hodgepodge of Reflections

a two-week holiday to visit with their relatives and friends.

Having retraced his steps to McChord Air Force Base, the moment Calvin stepped onto American soil, and boarded civilian flights, first to Atlanta, and from there to New York City, the quality of attention and respect he received from everyone with whom he interacted, proved both flattering and frustrating at the same time. He was not a little overwhelmed with feelings of indebtedness when a fellow-passenger traveling first class to New York gave up his seat to him so that he could enjoy the hospitalities that came with that class. The unaccustomed high regard for what he represented to the public at large, coupled with a sense of achievement having earned his medal, helped to diminish feelings of disappointment he was harboring, and that he experienced over his year of service as a soldier.

Even though Calvin, on his return to America, was wearing desert camio uniform and smelled like Iraq, he was slapped with the feeling of missing something, which he knew was his weapon. This feeling of nakedness lasted only a few days, in which time he hoped to have forgotten about Iraq, at least for the duration of his vacation. For him to truly relax and have fun, this would be imperative. Once out of the baggage-claim area, he spotted his taxi driver holding up a sign that said his name. This trip home would likely be the VIP-trip of his lifetime.

Calvin had not missed a military beat on his return to Iraq, this time around to FOB Marez, going into high gear the very next day when he and his peers were to go into the streets of Mosul, on what was called an "IED sweep', with the combat engineers.

On such a mission, the job of the combat engineer was to locate enemy-implanted IEDs (Improvised Exploding Devise), and to either defuse or blow them up. The job of the soldier was to tag along behind the engineers, providing security, and in the event of encountering reactionary forces, engage them in battle. On this sweep, four rocket launchers, two with rockets, were found and blown up by the combat engineers within the circle of guardian soldiers.

As if the day was not already sufficiently eventful, on the way home, Calvin identified the distinct sound of a car bomb explosion as they sped along a busy freeway through the city. Calvin was getting pretty good at identifying the sound of an explosion, whether it was made by mortar impact, a vehicle-borne IED, or a controlled detonation.

The daily occurrence of car bomb explosions were on the increase. They are not like those you see in the movies, where the car blows up and catches on fire. The Iraqi version leaves nothing of itself behind, only a hole in the ground where the car once stood. All is blown up into mushroom clouds of black smoke which can be seen several miles away, while the concussion of the blast spreads havoc to the surrounding area.

The first week after Calvin's return to Iraq, was highlighted by a Purple Heart Ceremony where his platoon sergeant received a Purple Heart medal for a bullet wound he received from an AK-47 at the hands of the enemy during a firefight. Calvin was touched by the whole proceedings of the ceremony, but grateful that he was not one of those receiving medals. To honor the wounded he thought, was good strategy. Not only was it an expression of appreciation for services rendered, and sympathy for injuries sustained, but more importantly, small encouragement to the soldier to continue the fight.

He returned to find himself caught up in a plot that was activated during his absence and that would force reluctant soldiers to write letters to their parents. Once a month, they were required to fill out postcards with messages to their parents, which were to be handed in to a supervisor for dispatch. Calvin detected the wisdom in this enforcement by the military. To keep parents informed about the condition of their child is good strategy. Parents need to know that their child is alive and well, and that his safety is a priority within the framework of war. It is important to the military to keep parents from becoming unduly worried and consequently opposed to the war. This letter-writing assurance, however, was not a problem for Calvin as he had always written regularly to his parents with comforting half-truths.

For Calvin, life was not all about fighting. He looked forward to his leisure time when he liked best to play volley ball at the base, before the court was closed due to a fatal attack on the lighting by a rocket-propelled grenade. He being the industrious type, took pleasure in cleaning his gun and gear, preparing his laundry list, itemizing articles of clothing up to twenty pieces and putting them in the green laundry bag to be sent to the wash on Thursdays at 0900. He took pleasure indulging his latest pastime of reading the independent, self-published blogs on the Internet. This he could do on one of the twenty Dell computers featured at the Morale, Welfare and Recreation (MWR) centre, for as long as he wished, (or for half an hour if there was someone waiting to use a computer). The blog postings of greatest interest to him, were those that shot off about follies of the U.S. military undertaking. Not that the bloggers would have been allowed to report on sensitive material, or to mention unflattering truths about the U.S. occupation without official intervention. What the blogger wrote had to be handed in for review, and await the green light before it could be posted.

Open twenty four hours a day, the MWR centre came equipped with a movie theatre that offered a daily midnight flick including free popcorn and Gatorade. If time permitted, Calvin would take in an occasional Hollywood blockbuster, such as Reds, starring Warren Beattie. Other entertainment opportunities provided at the MWR centre, included Xboxes, Play Stations, a Ping-Pong and Foosball tables, and a library with mostly trashy romance novels available on the honor system. Calvin found a connection to home, as well as a welcome escape from the reality of the war, by watching the news on Fox and CNN stations on the big-screen TV featured in the gym.

Preparations to hand over their equipment to their replacement, the 1st Infantry Division, were underway. Calvin would soon complete his two-year term

A Hodgepodge of Reflections

and, metaphorically speaking, come to the end of his rope. The knowledge of going home found him in a cheerful frame of mind. Being alive without physical injury, after having witnessed the deaths and maiming of a number of his comrades, left him feeling incredibly lucky.

The troops were brought together once more before their departure, and given a written examination that would reveal any sign of mental imbalance precipitated by the trauma of fighting a war. Yes-or-no type of questions enquiring into such things as changes in sleep pattern were asked. Despite a few ambiguous questions, Calvin soon grasped the aim behind the line of questioning and gave answers to them that would free him of the affliction of post-traumatic-stress syndrome. After the test, his platoon leader, explained to him the main purpose of the test, which was to protect the interest of the Army in the case where some sleazy veteran should launch a lawsuit against the Army, the recorded test results could serve as evidence.

Though frustration and drudgery dominated Calvin's mood, he would have been content to endure this state of mind if there was a glimmer of hope of a war to be won, or of an Iraqi people ready for democracy. Selling democracy to the Sunni Triangle was an idea that had been losing traction for some time, despite the handing over of stewardship of Iraq to the new Iraqi Interim Government, along with the creation of a new Iraqi Police force, an Army and an Iraqi Civil Defence Corps. This transition followed the official termination of the U.S. Coalition Provincial Authority on June 30 of 2004. The transition, however, had many inherent problems to be solved, and the kinks to be ironed out would take more than the luxury of time. One dilemma, for example, was the desertion of the force by a number of American-trained policemen and American-trained Iraqi Civil Defence Corps recruits, to cooperate with the enemy.

Calvin survived to witness some hearts being won locally, but the news from home was full of controversy and uncertainly concerning tenure of the U.S. occupation and success of the mission to Iraq. The escalation of insurgency was being matched by an increase in defensive action, thus a need for a change of intention from 'capture or kill' to 'kill or capture' was being voiced by the commanding component of the war machine.

At this point, the uncertainty concerning the potent question as to whether the insurgency was an anti-occupation movement, became yet another factor to contribute to Calvin's bag of mixed feelings. Never had this opinion been expressed openly at the governmental level. To express such an idea, would prompt easy solutions in public consciousness, that would be contrary to the purpose of the invasion. If getting out of Iraq would put an end to destruction and casualty, the solution to the problem would be to withdraw. Since the intent is to stay and to establish an imperialistic influence on Iraqi soil, mum would be the word that their presence is the cause of the insurgency and unrest.

In addition, the war was having the adverse effect of stirring up the eruptive animosity that existed between rival factions of Sunnis and Shiites. The likely development of civil war between the two great religious divisions of Islam, was a threat to the outcome of the American effort in Iraq. Words of caution voiced by scholars of the area, and disregarded by the Bush administration, as to the possibility of an outbreak of sectarian violence as an outcome of the invasion of Iraq, have returned to haunt the Administration.

The Americans came, and as it were, opened a cage door of a country of suppressed and basically disgruntled people, let them loose into a new freedom they knew not how to handle: into a state of panic and confusion, into a freshly destroyed infrastructure and an ensuing utter chaos. The people of Iraq, giving vent to feelings of escalating frustration and anger, pitted themselves against the invader, against each other, and inherently against their own best interest —- against the natural instinct for survival and eventful stabilization of the chaos — and, chose (for the significant part), retaliation and self-destruction.

Yet, there should be hope for a people unaccustomed to democracy, split by long-established rivalries, spinning out of control having lost the tightening grip of their autocratic leader that held them together under oppression. It should be the expectation that these people would surface from the quagmire to exhale, ultimately come to realize self-awareness, self-discovery and self-expression. This realization would serve to establish a social order to eliminate factional hostilities. Undoubtedly, this would be a slow process, which only the people themselves could bring about without the intervention of an occupying force. Not that outside assistance would not be appropriate, if not obligatory.

A general himself would be there at the 0900 formation at the mortar pool to reenlist those volunteers from amongst the troops who desired to renew their contracts to serve another term in Iraq with the American military. The general first gave a heartwarming speech to the willing reenlistees, after which he called them forwards and swore them in. But before dismissing the assembly he praised all participants for their admirable performances, and even gave some pointers to those that were leaving the force on how to conduct successful lives as veterans.

Calvin had grown contemptible toward what he deemed as hypocrisy in the general's speech. A speech which he thought reflected the speakers high intelligence and his specialized schooling in the craft of warfare, but which lacked insight into the folly, wastefulness and irrationality of the war venture. Was it that duty demanded his denial of his heartfelt feelings which he kept hidden under a cloak of hypocrisy?

Calvin stood solidly, if not alone, in disagreement with the general's concept of the war. It was as though they were looking at the same picture through different glasses, and the general's would have been the rose-colored ones. The general's concept embodying the idea that 'might is right', stank to high heavens. Would that the words uttered by the general had some bearing on the idea of a peaceful co-existence between nations of the earth, Calvin's single wish at that point would probably not

A Hodgepodge of Reflections

have been to return home to join forces with some peace-seeking movement.

It was at this turning point in his relatively short life that a distinction between intelligence and wisdom first dawned upon his youth. A wise person he thought, had to be one who was both intelligent as well as intellectual at the same time. An intellectual person had to be one who sought enlightenment through the acquisition of knowledge and, above all, an understanding of the human nature and its emotional needs and its anticicipated behavior under varying circumstances. But most importantly, and herein lay the crux of the matter, one who endeavored to demonstrate by his way of living, all the attributes that are attributable to the definition of wisdom, which list would indeed include such words as compassion and nonaggression. It must have been someone wise who came up with the saying that: 'a soft answer turneth away wrath.' Inquisitiveness into the history of past civilizations and the wars they forged, won or lost, could bring to the wise an awareness of the futility of war, and of the fact that only relatively seldom in history, had the response with force in dealing with any problem been warranted, nor indeed victorious.

Contemplating what he deemed might be sounding too much like a boy-scout-like approach, Calvin caught a hold of himself, toughened his opinion on the subject of war, by defending its limited usefulness only to the occasions of self-defense or in the defense of those threatened by a loss of life, or other extreme barbarity, having failed at all attempts at a nonviolent solution.

Wisdom too would fortify one with the knowledge that all members of the species Homo sapiens, regardless of their ethnic origin or nationality, share identical basic emotions when it comes down to brass tacks, and that it would be an error to assume that the differences in the behavior of others could be attributed to an innate inferiority or fault. Thus, a wise person would seek to understand the motivations behind the actions of the 'terrorist', and with this knowledge, seek to abate the anger behind his behavior.

Is it not curious too, that the millions of individuals that make up a nation should, with the exception of a paltry few, have the same response regarding the nature of the solution to a problem, such as that posed by the threat of terrorist attacks! Their behavioral response is akin to that of a school of fish, the individuals having learned in which direction to swim, all swim in that direction together. And the voice of the minority holding conflicting opinions is insufficient to influence the outcome of the popular vote determining the course of action.

Disregarding the facts that genetic traits are hereditary, and that mankind share common basic emotions, this sameness of attitude held by a nation regarding a course of action toward what they deem a provocation , must have passed down from generation to generation, from parents to their offsprings, and more incredibly, from placenta to fetus and mother's milk to infant, until it became an integral part of the whole. Would it be too much to expect that the consensus of opinion could have been derived from an honorable evaluation of the source of the provocation, and that a reaction would have been guided by wisdom?

The following question suggests plausibility of the argument made in the preceding paragraphs: why did the majority of the citizens of America choose a second time around to give continued support to the schoolyard-bullying tactics used by their government against a scapegoat of a country, even after it was revealed that the given reasons for picking that fight were based on a woven plot of deceptions that had actually met with some public disbelief and disapproval? The imbalance is not wholly explainable on the grounds of partisanship. And if this were the case, the picture would still be grim.

How can this integrated and erroneous set of values (take on conflict solving) be eradicated from the fabric of the peoples of the earth? Will the light that would replace illogicality with wisdom ever shine upon mankind? Will the day ever dawn upon us when military retaliation would become the last resort whenever a conflict between nations is to be settled? These may remain unanswered questions. Of all the peoples on earth, the Americans are the ones most suitable to lead by example!

So Calvin's thoughts digressed in his brain all the way home to New York, where he hoped to search out a political candidate who shared his ideal of nonaggression, if only such a one could be found in the U.S. of America. The one thing he was certain of was that there would be no simple solution to the problem, not unless of course, the solution to the problem was to be found in aggressive action.

Exposure to the woes and senseless disasters of war, over the two years Calvin spent in Iraq, had brought a change to certain concepts he once held about life and himself. His appreciation for peacetime, the living, life itself, and the simple commonplace things of life he used to take for granted, had heightened. To have witnessed the suffering of the less fortunate amongst the Iraqis, had the effect of deepening an awareness of his relative good fortune, thus, blunting the edge of his imperiousness. In contrast to his old self, he had grown more lenient toward imperfection in others and his environment. The internalized and punishing voice of his father that had turned him into a perfectionist, was losing its punch. The following poem speaks for itself:

He joined the army in answer to a calling

And like a medal, he wore his call to duty.

Into Iraq,

In search of weapons of mass destruction, he waded through the ruins,

But only the dead did he find there.

A Hodgepodge of Reflections

Into Iraq,

In search of biological warfare —— or he who would oppose ——

He forced his entry through many a door

But only the panic-stricken, did he find there.

He loaded his gun in the name of freedom

And emptied its contents into a crowd

One gasped, and found freedom in his death.

The smoke from his gun mushroomed into a cloud of mixed emotions

Obscuring his vision —— the purpose of his mission:

There were no embraces for the liberator! And

No 'Lady Democracy' to be seen on the horizon.